Queenie knew starting a new romance in late September was a bad idea, but without Mitch Kingsolver, her fledgeling business, *Queen of Tarts,* would never have been so successful. When October comes, Queenie's life is swallowed up in what she knows as the Caledonian Curse, when a cranky Scotswoman persona takes her over all the way to Halloween. Hiding away is the only way Queenie knows to deal with the Curse, but she had hoped Mitch would support her. Instead, Mitch has vanished, and Queenie has to deal with a not-quite-stranger. When she first met James Stuart, she thought he was her ideal man, but James and Mitch are inextricably entwined. It's up to Queenie, burdened as she is, to get James to the Halloween Ball and hope she can unravel the mess. Dressed as the Queen of Tarts, Queenie has just one chance to make it work for them all.

This book is a work of fiction. Names, characters, places, and incidents either are products of the author's imagination or are used fictitiously. Any resemblance to actual events or locales or persons, living or dead, is entirely coincidental.

Queen of Tarts 2
Copyright © 2021 Lark Westerly
ISBN: 978-1-4874-3454-0
Cover art by Martine Jardin

Published by eXtasy Books Inc

Look for us online at:
www.eXtasybooks.com

Queen of Tarts 2
A Fairy in the Bed

By

Lark Westerly

DEDICATION

For everyone who tries to be better — let's all put more love in the world. It needs everything we can give.

AUTHOR'S NOTE

The *Fairy in the Bed* series features a sprawling cast of characters who wander in and out of one another's stories.

Queenie Hart is a new character, but you might recognise some of the supporting players from other books in the series.

Queen of Tarts takes place in 2020 and 2021, but for the purposes of this story, the Covid 19 epidemic never happened. After all, it's not *quite* our world.

For more about this series, visit Lark's website at https://larksinger.weebly.com

CHAPTER ONE: EMBROIDERY

Jacaranda Fairling, October 25th, 2021

Jacaranda Fairling thought she probably shouldn't have agreed to make a costume for the startling young woman who came into her shop, Fairings, speaking with a wildly inaccurate Scottish accent that ebbed and flowed erratically.

The improbably named Queenie Hart wanted to attend a Halloween Ball in the persona of her luxury pastry business . . . the Queen of Tarts.

Jacaranda's friend and business partner, Lucida, had wanted Queenie to have her costume, and so it was agreed.

There was a great deal of work on hand, and Jacaranda and Lucida had to work overtime to get the costume done.

Without discussion, for they had worked together for twenty-five years, Jacaranda and Lu had launched into their respective specialities. Jacaranda took down bales of blueberry, raspberry red, and marmalade gold velvet brocade. Then she went to her treasure chest for remnants in royal blue, angelica green, and biscuit silk.

She laid out her fabrics and cut out the pattern, with the skirt calf-length at the back and short at the front. She cut the deep bodice and handed each piece to her partner, who was already sorting her silks.

"Do your magic, Lu," she said.

Lucida stretched a piece of fabric, seemingly at random, on her embroidery hoop and threaded up a needle with glittering floss.

Jacaranda returned to her cutting and began to baste the pieces together on a dressmaker's form.

She glanced at Lucida's work, and as always, she marvelled at the magical design growing under her partner's clever fingers. Glowing tarts tumbled down the length of the skirt, and the front panel of the bodice glittered with an elaborate jewelled crown.

Lucida took up another panel and began on a riot of twining flowers, possibly morning glories. A white stag peeped through the floral thicket, and a design of three linked hearts embraced the décolletage.

More and more symbols and pictures appeared, and Jacaranda forced her mesmerised gaze back to her own work.

With the cutting and the shaping completed, she turned her attention to six simple costumes for their own party — because, with Lucida in full flight, there was no *way* the ladies of Fairings were going to miss seeing the effect of the Queen of Tarts at the Fiddle Bay Halloween Ball.

Chapter Two: Aide-Mémoire

Queenie Hart, Late September, 2021

Queenie Hart woke with a start and stretched out her hand. She was alone in the bed.

She sat up, feeling bereft, and saw a breakfast tray on her nightstand. It bore brown bread and cheese, and a pink grapefruit with a silver spoon she didn't recognise. An envelope was propped against a glass of apple juice with a strawberry slotted over the rim.

Queenie opened it and found a printed photograph of a smiling young man in a dull green shirt. She frowned. He looked lovely, but she had no sense of knowing him.

Don't be daft, lassie. Ye ken fine who that must be.

She woke her phone and looked at a photo in her gallery, comparing the two.

The bus driver. The delivery man. The Fixer. Mitchell Kingsolver. My friend, and now my lover.

Except that she paid him.

But she hadn't paid him for the last few times he'd driven her to and from the market stall at the festival.

Or had she?

Bedding the Queen of Tarts must be expensive.

He'd said that, or something like it, as a joke, and he'd apologised after she'd unleashed a stream of what an admiring bystander had dubbed *lassie haggis* at him.

And she *did* trade as the Queen of Tarts, with a steady stream of orders for her luxury tarts.

But . . . *Bedding the Queen of Tarts?*

I enjoyed it at least as much as he did. I invited him. And he said *he was here because he wanted to be. He was lovely to me.*

The envelope had a ridge in it, so she slid her fingers in and pulled out his pen — a distinctive implement made of polished bamboo-like wood. It had a strip of paper wrapped around it in a spiral.

Queenie unwound it and flattened it out.

Not assuming anything, my love, but I suggest you write an aide-mémoire *to remind you of who the photo represents. I wouldn't want you to suppose you have photos of random men on your breakfast tray. By the way, it's a portrait of me — Mitchell Kingsolver. I hope you'll look at it often when I'm not able to be with you. XOX*

Queenie frowned.

He could have written on it himself.

She turned the photo face up and wrote across the pale shirt . . .

Mitchell Kingsolver

I should frame it and keep it by the bed. Or is that assuming too much?

Why on earth she couldn't remember his face when he wasn't in front of her was a puzzle neither of them could solve. Mitch didn't seem too troubled, but Queenie went through agonies about it. It was bad enough that she had to spend the month of October speaking cod Scottish and making herself unpopular, and worst of all, having to guard against spending her small nest egg on inappropriate Scottish luxuries and peculiar ethnic trifles.

She'd lately learned that her affliction was probably a manifestation, or second self, a legacy from the small percentage of fay blood in her veins.

Until the month before, she had known almost nothing about the fay, but her father's half-fay cousin and his wife had explained some things to her. Her new landlords at

Porthwellian Tredennick had explained more, and the housewarming present they had sent her, a set of books called *Orders of the Fay* and *The Fay Companion,* had proved a mine of information.

Knowing what the Caledonian Curse probably was didn't help her to solve its problems, however.

She *must* tell Mitch about the Curse.

She was amazed he hadn't questioned her about it already. Normally, it hit on October the first. This year, it was getting in early.

She ate her breakfast and showered.

Mitch's note had not mentioned if or when he was coming back to The Belfry, although the gift of the photograph and the affectionate closing line on his note implied he would see her soon, and often.

She hoped so.

Queenie, unwilling to wait in a lovelorn manner, employed herself by sorting out the aftermath of the Oakengrove Festival.

She already had the new orders in sequence, so she went to inspect her stores.

Time to start baking.

She made a batch of Raspberry Relish for the remainder of Oliver Porthwellian's order, and she added an extra-large Queen of Hearts as a sorry-present for being late. He could slice it up and eat a piece every now and again.

Oliver was ninety-six. He was one of her landlords, and he lived in Victoria. Because he was a pisky man — the same order of fairy as her dad's Cousin Branok and his wife — he was able to conjure items to and from his old home at The Belfry. He had startled Queenie very much when he'd conjured the lease agreement.

His talent was useful when it came to delivering his orders for tarts. He had Queenie put them in a big tureen and leave them on a table at an agreed time.

This morning, his tureen was waiting in the usual place, with a tart little note suggesting savouries were tasty but a man of his age enjoyed the sweeter things of life.

Queenie wrote a note back to inform him she was about to experiment with currants, as he had suggested in one of his notes. She asked whether he meant the small, dried grapes usually sold as *currants* or true currants of the Ribes genus . . . and if so, whether he wanted red, black, or white. *I wish to please, not to annoy,* she added, *and the Ribes tribe is not known for sweetness.*

The tureen remained where it was for a few hours and then vanished. It reappeared twenty minutes later with a new note from Oliver, written in his cultured hand with his dip pen.

Surprise me.

Queenie rolled her eyes.

Men and their cryptic notes!

She would make tarts using some of each.

She didn't have true currants to hand, and she doubted if the small independent supermarket, Fiddle-de-Dee, stocked them in any case.

She telephoned the Fixer, who had helped her immeasurably already.

"Fixer."

"It's me, Queenie Hart. I'm in a fix."

"Another one?"

She heard the smile in his voice, and, as she had the photograph in her hand, she could match a face to the voice.

She wasn't even trying to delude herself she'd called him for any reason other than to remind him of their night together and to entice him to return.

"Aye. One of my customers wants currant tarts, and I don't know where to source true currants."

"Fresh or dried?"

"Either."

"Fresh might not be available so early in the season, but I

know someone who grows and dries her own. I'm sure she'd be happy to supply you."

"How much?"

"Would a kilogram of mixed ones do?"

"No, ye randy haggis. I mean, *how much do they cost.*"

"Randy haggis. That's a new one. I like it. You be my Queen of Tarts forever, and I'll be your Randy Haggis whenever I can."

He was flirting with her. She quite liked that.

Some men dropped the flirting when they'd got what they presumably wanted. Mitch was going the other way around.

He went on, "She doesn't have much use for money, but she'll consider herself well-recompensed when I explain who they're for."

"Why? I assume she doesn't know me?"

"No, but she loves me dearly, and she will regard a favour for you as a gift for me."

Queenie was startled. If he meant what it sounded like, this was a long way beyond flirting. It was practically a declaration of intention.

"It's what I do," he added.

Oh. He needs to fix — to help — and this facilitates that.

"This someone is your mother, I take it."

"Yes." The love was very evident in his voice. "Danna Kingsolver is my mother, and the best a man could have."

"You're her favourite son?"

There was a small pause, as if she hadn't made the quip, and then he continued, "How soon do you need the currants, love?"

"When you can manage it."

"Say — nine o'clock, then?"

"What — tonight?"

"Yes, unless that's too soon."

"Not too soon. You're welcome to stay for supper — and for breakfast."

7

There, she'd said it.

"I would love to more than I can say, but I can't leave Ayesha overnight again so soon. She dislikes disruptions and she knows when one is coming."

Queenie felt snubbed. It could be true, but it could also be that his ice queen of a cat, Ayesha, if she existed at all, was a convenient distancing technique.

"Raincheck?" he said.

"If you want." She tried to sound casual.

"I want one, but it's also about what *you* want, love."

"I want you to come for supper and bed when it's convenient to you—and to Ayesha. Is that plain enough?"

"Perfectly. I'm longing for it, and for you. If I could, I'd spend every night with you for as long as we live."

"You—"

He'd hung up.

Queenie growled.

Every night wi' me. If he could. What's stopping him? A cat!

Then, feeling out of sorts, she telephoned the only other person she could think of to annoy.

CHAPTER THREE: ADVICE

Queenie Hart, Late September, 2021

"Greetings, Queenie Hart," the cheerful voice answered her from a thousand kilometres away.

Queenie frowned. "What happened to *Porthwellian Tredennick. Androw Tredennick speaking?*"

"I put your number in the memory to save time," the junior partner of the firm who were her landlords said. "What can I do for you? Is Oliver being obnoxious about the cheese tarts you sent him?"

"No."

"Just as well, since the speed with which he ate them all means he has no right to criticise them. What's wrong, then?"

Queenie realised she wasn't sure what to say. Nothing was wrong . . . well, nothing *he* could cure. She'd rung because she wanted someone to vent to and because Andy always answered the phone.

Andy was waiting, so she pulled herself together. "You're married."

"Entirely. Faithfully. Joyfully. Permanently." His voice had cooled a shade.

"But if you weren't — when you weren't — what would you be implying if you asked a woman for a raincheck?"

"I never did that. Never had reason to."

"If you had."

"If my miss — my Dellion — had ever offered me anything I couldn't accept that instant, I'd have asked for a raincheck and I'd have cashed it in as soon as I could, with a bunch of flowers for her trouble."

"What if you hadn't wanted what was on offer, and were just being polite?"

A scuffle heralded Dellion's inevitable arrival. "Oh, he'd have wanted it, sweet. He always wants it."

"Wants what? What's she talking about?" Andy asked *sotto voce.*

"Whatever I have to offer is what you always want and always get. Shove over, Andy. In fact, go away. I want to talk to Queenie."

After a bit more scuffling Dellion said, "There, he's gone. What's going on, sweet? Who have you offered what to, and why did he ask for a raincheck?"

Queenie said, "Do you know a man called Mitchell Kingsolver, Dellion?"

"No. I'd remember a name like that. Is there any reason why I should know him?"

"Probably not. He's a bus driver. And a delivery man for the supermarket. And he fixes problems for people. He's the one who brought me and my stuff to The Belfry when the moving companies wouldn't help. They wanted me to wait for days and days. He came to me in a couple of hours."

"Oh. You mean he's a fix-it pixie?"

"A what?"

"Is he a fix-it pixie?"

"A—" It sounded like something from a children's television program.

In a fix, then Mitch'll fix it . . .

Dellion's voice interrupted her mental jingle. "Read your housewarming present. Look under Pixies in volume four and you'll find a sub-section about manifestations and oddities exclusive to that order. They have a few, including one or two they barely believe in themselves until they're forced to."

"Oh. But aren't pixies . . ."

Little skippy beings, she was about to say, but that was non-sense. Fairies . . . the ones she had met . . . were people, with different skills, social mores, and better health than humans. She remembered how cranky her dad's cousin, Branok St Ives, had been when she'd flippantly referred to green blood.

He'd informed her sharply that his blood was red, and that he could so handle cold iron.

Dellion giggled. "Pixies are similar to us piskies, sweetie, but most people say they're a wee bit more user-friendly. Look them up in your book, but before you do that, tell me — what on earth did you offer yours that he didn't grab with both hands? Pixies are as sexy as hell . . . nearly as hot as we are."

Queenie said, "On Saturday night, he brought me back from a festival at Oakengrove where I was selling tarts. He'd been driving people about all day, and we were both tired out. He stayed for supper and . . ."

"And for horizontal dessert," Dellion supplied.

"There wasn't any dessert. We slept."

"There was horizontalism, though. In proximity. In a bed."

"Yes."

"Was that the first time you'd got horizontal with him?"

"Yes."

"Then if you were both tired, it's a good thing there was no dessert, because you both might have been disappointed. Was he nice to you, otherwise? Or did he hog the bed and keep poking you as if he thought you might not be ripe? You can learn a lot about men from the way they act in bed."

"He stayed on his own side of the bed I expect. I was asleep. He brought me breakfast and a daffodil."

"Well-done-him. Obviously, he's nice to look at. Pixies are. But which type is he? Green eyes? Brown? How olive? Does he rub up green?"

Queenie, flummoxed by the flurry of questions she either

couldn't answer or didn't understand, hurried to the bedroom and looked at the picture Mitch had left for her. She had
one in her phone, but she didn't want to risk poking about in
the gallery while she was having a conversation in case she X-
ed out of the call. "Yes," she said.

"Yes to what?"

"Nice to look at. Lovely, in fact."

"That's a given, but it took you long enough to decide."

"I had to check his photo. I can never remember his face
when he's not here in front of me."

Dellion whistled thoughtfully through her teeth. "Never
heard of that one before. Sounds like a wish-gone-south to
me. Does he smell nice?"

"Yes. Like blue gums after rain."

"So what's the problem with your raincheck? Whyever
would he need a raincheck?"

"I went to the festival again yesterday, and Mitch brought
me back and he stayed for supper again."

"Supper and . . . and this time I'm guessing you got to have
dessert."

"Yes."

"So I'm guessing you invited him for a rerun tonight, and
he said he had a previous engagement."

"Yes. With a cat named Ayesha."

"But he still asked for a raincheck."

"Yes. And he's coming to bring me some currants for my
baking at nine tonight. *Nine tonight.* That sounded like a prop-
osition to me, but when I tried to take him up on it, he started
in with the raincheck, about how Ayesha hates to be disrupted and how she knows when a disruption is coming."

"Sounds unusually needy for a cat."

"Yes, especially as he previously said she generally didn't
care if he was there or not," Queenie said sourly.

"If he's coming to visit you at nine, I suggest you ask him

if he'd like to skip supper and go straight for dessert and then go home to Ayesha afterwards. If he lights up and says *yes,* then you'll know he's telling the literal truth. He almost certainly is. Pixies are fearfully honest."

"Aren't piskies?"

"Ye-es . . . but we believe in *spin.* Pixies don't. And Queenie . . ."

"Yes?"

"When you've had it — had *him* — and you've got to the sleepy snuggling stage, make sure you get him up and send him home to Ayesha spit-spot. That way he'll know you respect his wishes — and his cat's needs — and you're not trying to be subversive and manipulative and tempt him into staying. Unless you are trying to do that, naturally."

"I'm not. I'm just trying to work him out."

"Then ask him nicely if he'd like to enjoy you for dessert. And if he still says no, then you'll have to respect that too. They say men are governed by their willies, and a lot of them are — go *away* Andy — I'm talking to Queenie. Where was I — yes, well, they *are.* It's a biological urge, and it's fun to tease them. But the best men, and *I* have one of those for my exclusive pleasure — *Andy, I said to go* — they can think of other things such as duty and promises and right-and-good behaviour even if they do have an insistent willy trying to rule the roost. If your Master Kingsolver is one of those good ones, then he'll be ever so happy to have his tart and eat it too."

"What?"

"I mean, when you show him he can have you for dessert and still attend to his obligation to his cat, he'll be pleased. And now Andy's trying to get hold of the phone, and I'd better let him, or I won't get *my* dessert tonight."

Andy came back on the line. "My wife doesn't know the meaning of the word *appropriate,* but I hope her advice was of some use."

"I think it was verra useful — but I need a bit more, from you."

"I hope it's nothing to do with horizontal dessert, because I can't, and I won't, discuss that with you. Especially after that question about my little brother."

Queenie sighed. When she'd first met Andy, if holding conversations over the phone could be described as *meeting,* she'd asked him if he had an available, unmarried brother. It had slipped out because she liked him so much and had just discovered he was married. Andy had informed her that he did have a single brother, but that he was a child of nine.

Queenie wished she'd kept her mouth shut.

She said, "It's nothing to do with that. It's about the Caledonian Curse. The Halloween manifestation. It's coming in early, and soon I'll have to go into hermit mode to avoid ruining friendships or getting myself arrested or ostracised. I can manage the isolation, but if Mitch and I are — well, enjoying regular dessert — what will he think if I tell him I can't see him for a month?"

Andy didn't answer immediately, and when he did, he didn't rush in with assurances. Finally, he said, "Why not tell him about the manifestation and let him choose whether he can handle being called a — well, whatever — in the heat of the moment?"

"I suppose I could, but the lassie haggis babble isn't the half of it. I'm afraid I'll spend my nest egg on something unsuitable or seduce a passing Scotsman . . . and from what Dellion said, that might not go down well with Mitch. I'm really not *like* that — except in October, or when I'm under unusual stress."

"I can't save the Scotsman's virtue, but I *can* help with the nest egg problem."

"Oh?"

"Since you don't need it for rent next month, why not put

it into the hands of someone you trust for a few weeks? We could handle it here, but your cousin would be a better choice, since you know him and he's in the same state. He also knows about your specific problem—in fact, he identified it, right?"

Queenie found she was nodding slowly. It made sense. She probably should visit Branok and Gillan anyway, to thank them again for their help before the Caledonian Curse took her over. "I will. Thanks, Andy. And thank Dellion for me."

"Okay. By the way, what's lassie haggis?"

Queenie chuckled and explained.

"Most apt," Andy said dryly. "*Nos da.*" He hung up.

Queenie telephoned Branok St Ives and made an appointment for the next day. Time was short, and she was glad he had agreed to see her in the morning. Then she returned to her baking.

At seven-thirty, she tidied the kitchen and sat down with Volume 4 of *Orders of the Fay* which she read with one hand while eating supper with the other.

It was enlightening, and she wished she'd read it thoroughly before. Despite what Dellion had said about pixies being user-friendly, it seemed there were several pitfalls for the unwary woman who loved one.

When she heard the mini-bus pull up outside, she put aside the book and hurried to the door, holding Mitch's photo in her hand.

She opened the door quickly, swapped her gaze from the picture to his face and then put her arms around him, bringing his head down for a kiss.

Something hard dug into her ribs for a few seconds and then vanished, and he put both arms around her in a fervent hug. One hand headed south and cupped her bottom in a possessive fashion.

They kissed for a while longer and then he lifted his head and smiled down at her.

"Love, that was the best greeting I've ever had."

"Aye, laddie, it was the best greeting I ever gave!" she said breathlessly. She went on, "I know you just came to drop off the currants, and I know you have to get back to Ayesha, but if you have half an hour to spare, I'd like to take you to bed."

He bent to kiss her again. "I have an hour and I can't think of another way I'd rather spend it. Shall we?"

"Aye!" She disengaged and took his hand. Then she gave him a puzzled look. "Did you bring the currants?"

"They're in your kitchen."

He hasn't been in the kitchen yet.

She laughed. "Of course they are. It's what you do."

The explanation for his lightning speed was so simple now she'd followed Dellion's directive and paid attention to her housewarming gift.

She really should have worked it out before.

Oliver Porthwellian was able to shift things according to his will because he was a fairy man—a pisky. It was now perfectly clear to Queenie that Mitch could load and unload his bus, shift groceries, fetch soup from his *pied-a-terre* in Borrowdale Junction and offer to provide forgotten ingredients because he was a fairy man too. His ears weren't pointed because he wasn't a pisky like the few fairy people whose order she knew for sure. He was a pixie with a fix-it manifest. He had a natural desire to *fix* things, and so he'd made a living and a vocation out of doing what he would have done anyway.

He'd been telling her so from the start in an oblique kind of way.

It followed that he'd understand about the Caledonian Curse . . . or at least he wouldn't think it was as bizarre or as perverse as her ex-boyfriends and her parents, her neighbour, and her ex-employers had. She'd have to explain it to him *soon.* Tomorrow . . . Thursday at the *very* latest.

Maybe—surely—he'd understand, and he'd know she

couldn't help it. When they reached the bedroom, Queenie dropped her gown to reveal what she had underneath . . . which was nothing.

Mitch's eyes lit up with a sparkle of desire.

"Go on, get naked," she said softly.

He raised his hands to unbutton his blue shirt.

She reached out to stop him. "The other way. The unload-the-supplies way. It's quicker. I want to watch you do it."

His smile widened. He lifted one hand and quickly double tapped the opposite wrist. His clothing vanished.

Queenie looked him over appreciatively. "You really are ready!"

"Yes, but I can wait until you are."

"I am."

"I've been waiting for you all my life, I think, and I wish I'd met you earlier," he said.

She stepped up close and put her arms around him, unbalancing them so they toppled onto the bed.

In a quick scramble, they were coupled up and kissing.

Queenie released his mouth just long enough to say, "You will hold hard?"

"I always do."

It was one more thing she'd read that had fallen into place. Fairy men carried no disease, and they never needed to use contraceptives, since conception was a matter of choice for the fay. *Hold hard* was the term they used for consciously *not* planting a baby.

She wrapped her legs more tightly around him. Too soon, she felt her vision blurring and she cried out. This time, she resisted her urge to go limp, and she kept moving until he relaxed and let out a long sigh.

He handed her a soft cloth.

"You came prepared?"

"I—hoped. I didn't expect. I thought you might be miffed

with me over the silly joke I made."

"I hoped too—after I got over being miffed."

He put his arms around her again.

"Just stay a wee while and then you need to go home to mollify your moggy," she murmured.

"Thank you for understanding." He kissed her neck.

We ought to have that talk, now, tonight, Queenie thought. She drew breath to tell him about the Curse, but he went on kissing her and she wanted to concentrate on feeling . . . wanted. And valued. And loved. She did feel loved, and it was intoxicating.

Just a wee bit longer. Queenie wanted to ask him for that, but it would be unfair. It would also be unwise. He might love her, but he also had to feel he could trust her.

Their hour was almost up, and she sat up reluctantly and swung her legs out of bed. Then she leaned down and kissed Mitch's cheek.

"Ayesha awaits with claws at the ready. Or is she the cold offended kind who turns her back and makes her shoulder-blades look dangerous?"

"That one." He gave her his quick grin and sat up. "I don't want to leave you, my beautiful Queen of Tarts. If I had my way, I'd never spend a night away from you again. Meeting you, loving you, is the best thing I've ever done."

"I'd love to spend my nights with you, too. I don't want you to leave, but I know you have to go now. I'll get dressed and give you your tarts."

"Am I due for some tarts? I thought I just had the queen of them all."

"Ah-ah," she reproved him. "Ye don't get me that way a second time, laddie." She caught herself up as Caledonia rolled on her tongue. "Yes, you're due for tarts. You brought me currants, remember?"

"Those are a gift from Mum."

"You can give her the tarts, then. Or I'll give you twice as many and you can share. I always pay my debts."

He got out of bed.

Queenie kept looking at him. He had unblemished olive skin all over. He was beautiful.

Dellion had said something about *rubbing up green,* and she'd read about that, too. Male pixies could make their skin go green—or at least more olive—by rubbing a pulse point.

She remembered him rubbing his wrist with his thumb, just before she took his hands for the first time. What was that about? Had he been trying to show her what he was without saying it in so many words? Or had he been thinking about conjuring something, or even about the possibility of undressing?

Lawks! What if he'd gone naked right there in my kitchen!

"If you keep looking at me like that I'll want to get back into your bed and stay forever," he said.

"How was I looking?"

"As if you had designs on me."

"I do." She turned around and pulled on her gown. By the time she had the sash tied, Mitch was dressed again, buttons and all. He held out his arms.

She went into them.

"You're not staring at my face, my love. Are you starting to remember it?"

"No, but I know your voice, and the way you smell."

"Medicinal," he said.

"Not a bit. You smell like a eucalyptus forest after rain. I love it." She wouldn't say *I love you.* Not quite yet. Maybe not until after they'd weathered the depths and extent of the Caledonian Curse. If he still wanted her when he'd seen and heard the worst of her, then she'd say it with pleasure.

"You smell like tarts."

She rubbed her face against his collar. "That's because I've been baking, but yours is a *bouquet des fees,* is that right?"

19

She felt him stiffen. "Have you been talking to someone about me?"

She wondered if it was her imagination, but the warmth in his voice seemed to have faded.

She faced it head-on. "Yes—but I also have a kind of encyclopaedia my landlords sent me. That was nothing to do with you. They don't know you. It was housewarming gift."

"I see."

"It's called *The Orders of the Fay* and it's fascinating. It explains all kind of things about folk like you."

"Folk like me."

His voice *was* cool. She wasn't imagining it.

"Why didn't you tell me you were a fairy with a manifestation?"

He was quiet for so long, she thought he wasn't going to answer. Then he said, "Does it matter to you what I am?"

"No' that you're a fairy, but—ye could hae told me what you were."

"Well, I didn't feel like it. How much of that book have you read?"

"Quite a bit. I read up about manifestations, and conjuring . . . It explains so much I never understood about you before," she said.

"I see."

She retreated from his arms. "I'll go and get your tarts."

She packed a selection into a box and eyed the snap-lock container on the bench. Currants from his mum, she supposed.

Mitch came in behind her and she turned and looked anxiously into his face, learning it again. "Do you—or your mum—need the container back right now?"

He shook his head. "Any time will do. May I?" He held out his hand, and she gave him the box.

"I have some deliveries to do tomorrow, but I'll come to

see you as soon as I can. I have some things you need to hear."

"I'll be in Sydney tomorrow," she said.

"What for?"

"I'm going to see my cousin."

"Can you put it off for a few days? I need to talk to you."

Queenie frowned. She didn't feel like telling him about her problem with money. He'd think she was stupid. And with the Curse hovering so close she could almost see its dark wings, she was suddenly desperate to get her savings somewhere safe.

"If we're going to be together, it's important that we talk as soon as possible," he said.

Queenie said coolly, "It can't be all that urgent. You've been here for an hour. You could have said whatever you needed to tonight."

"As I recall it, *someone* swept me off to bed for a steamy session, so I didn't get a chance."

They stared at one another.

Mitch's olive face had gone sallow. His beautiful eyes looked like a cornered cat's.

"That was a verra low blow," Queenie said.

"It was. I apologise unreservedly. I'll come and pick you up from here in the morning and take you to the junction. Better yet, I'll drive you to Sydney myself. We'll talk on the way."

"What about the bus service? You can't leave folk stranded."

"There are always taxis."

"Don't be ridiculous. People depend on you. You can't possibly let anyone down. You're hardwired not to."

"Believe me, I don't ever want to let anyone down. I make whatever provision I can to avoid it, but sometimes I just can't. I especially can't bear to let you down. Queenie, *please* put your cousin off. Or, if you must go to the city, I'll drive you."

"I can perfectly well take the train. I'll walk to the post office in the morning and meet the bus there. I'll see you then." She turned and led the way to the door, closing off to the peculiar conversation. "Goodnight, Mitch . . .no, don't keep arguing. You're in a rush to get home to your cat, remember?"

He stared at her helplessly for a few seconds, then he bent and kissed her cheek. "Goodnight, Queenie."

She watched him walk into the darkness, heading for his bus and the exacting Ayesha.

CHAPTER FOUR: NEST EGG

Queenie Hart, Late September, 2021

Queenie slept badly, but she thought she'd feel better when she had her finances made safe. She still had a couple of days to sort things out with Mitch.

He'd been impatient and unreasonable.

She'd been hasty and implacable.

They'd sort it out. It was just a part of becoming a couple. One day, they'd laugh about it.

She reached out in the bed, rolling her face in the pillow, which still held his fresh scent.

In the morning, she walked into Fiddle Bay. She was beginning to know some of the locals. In her mind she associated them with the tarts they preferred. Harriet Charming, the woman with the bicycle, cycled by and raised a hand in greeting. *Strawberry Hearts.*

A white-haired woman, hand-in-hand with a compact Mediterranean-looking man of the same age, blew her a kiss. "Thank you for the tarts, my love!"

Queenie couldn't remember serving her, but she had seen the couple at Oakengrove, shepherding a shy-looking teenager.

Duncan Dee from the supermarket flicked her a wave as she passed. Well may he, she thought. She was probably one of his best bulk customers by now. He liked the Raspberry Relish tarts, which were Oliver Porthwellian's favourites, too.

A group of senior citizens sat around a table on the village green, playing chess. One of her expandable tart boxes graced the table, along with a jug of something with orange slices on the rim.

She caught the bus at the post office. After travelling with Mitch from Sydney and to and from markets, it seemed odd to revert to being one passenger among several.

She said *good morning* as she boarded the bus and handed the driver the fare. She wasn't holding her *aide-mémoire,* so she just had to trust the driver was Mitch. She focused on his hands, and recognition swept over her. Those hands had held her last night. She'd kissed him and made love with him and longed for him to stay.

But he'd gone cool on her . . . and hadn't he amused himself by giving her hints?

Well, I didn't feel like it. He'd sounded offhand — dismissive, even — when she asked why he hadn't told her what he was.

She was unsure why this hurt her so much.

And then there was all that palaver about coming to see her at lunchtime today. And wanting her to put off her own affairs to suit him. And wanting to drive her to Sydney.

She watched him help other passengers, sometimes overtly, and sometimes secretly. More than once she caught him conjuring some awkward article into place, and possibly taking some of the weight for a burdened elder. No one else noticed, or, if they did, they took it for granted as something Mitch the driver did.

At Borrowdale Junction, he helped two elderly passengers down from Ethel, which was the name he'd given his green-painted mini-bus, and carried their cases to the train, chatting away as if they were his favourite great-uncles.

He's so considerate.

Mentally, she slapped her fingers.

He's just doing what he has to do — just as you have to gabble lassie haggis and try to buy clan tartans from the Outer Hebrides. He's acting the way he's programmed to. He's a fix-it pixie . . .

Lordie, how twee is that?

She disembarked quickly and walked to the train. She passed a couple of tall young men coming back towards Ethel. One of them was probably Mitch, but which one? They both wore blue cords and polo shirts.

Ah! One of them glanced at her, paused and looked again, apparently admiring her cleavage.

Not Mitch. He looks at my face, first.

She looked at the other one. He caught her worried gaze, and he put a cap she would swear he hadn't been holding on his head. *Driver.*

"It's me, Queenie, love." His voice was warm and pleading.

She bit her lip, wanting to reach for him and breathe in his lovely clean scent.

"Please, *please* . . . won't you let me drive you to your cousin's?" he asked humbly.

"No. You have work to do here."

"Then I'll see you when you come back."

She nodded.

Later, she sat in the train, staring at the photo in her phone.

How could I ever forget your face?

But she knew she would as soon as the screen went dark.

Why can't I remember you?

Why didn't I say yes *to you?*

It was just a few weeks since she'd left the city, but plunging back into the busy streets felt claustrophobic.

She walked five blocks to the high-rise where Branok St Ives had his office and stepped in.

Reception and the outer office were untenanted, so she called out, "Branok?"

The door to the inner office swung open.

He conjured that.

Queenie entered the main office and then went through to the sitting room.

Branok was at a desk that hadn't been there before. The black spaniel bitch lay nearby, with her chin resting on Branok's foot.

They both looked up, and the dog snuffed the air with sudden eagerness.

"Greetings, Queenie." Branok gave her his quick smile. He was four years younger than her dad, whose cousin he was, and nothing like him. He was fit-looking, with strong features, dark hair, and clothing that sparkled with zippers. He had a short silver earring in one lobe.

From her close reading of *The Fay Companion,* Queenie now knew that the short earring proclaimed his married state, and the two silver rings on his right hand represented his two sons. Each ring sparkled with a tiny jewel . . . grandchildren.

She said, "Hi, Branok . . . Lady Velvet. I see *you* smell tarts."

"I suspect we both can, and possibly we're both hoping for a chance to sample them," Branok said.

Queenie crossed the room and sat down in the chair she'd occupied before, by the small kitchen.

Branok raised one brow, got up and walked across to sit opposite to her on the couch.

He and her dad, Shane, didn't get on, so she had met him just a handful of times. Since he and his wife had recommended her for her new home in Kirk Circle, she was disposed to be grateful to him.

That didn't mean she would let him get away with lording over her—if that was what he was doing. According to Dellion Tredennick, who was in a position to know, piskies usually had an angle.

"May I have a cup of tea to go with the tarts?" Queenie asked. She'd been too distracted by the situation with Mitch to eat breakfast at The Belfry.

If Branok found that request out of order she couldn't tell. "I'm sure Gillan will get us one. I trust nothing's wrong at your new home, Cousin Queenie?"

"Nothing's really wrong — at least, nothing new. And nothing at all's wrong with The Belfry, beyond an occasional rustle which might be birds on the roof. I love it. It's perfect. I can't thank you enough for recommending me for an inheritance property."

Branok relaxed a bit. "Nothing creepy about it, then?"

"Nothing at all, truly. It's a lovely place. Things tend to vanish and reappear, but that's not creepy. That's Oliver Porthwellian."

"*Oh?*"

"Don't tell me that old coot's still above ground," Gillan's voice said from the kitchen.

Queenie jumped.

"Don't do that, Gill, you're scaring Queenie," Branok said.

"You *asked* me for tea." Gillan came over and sat next to him. She had on a ruby-coloured dress that accentuated her handsome features and dark colouring. Her plethora of silver chains and charms shone against the plain background and picked up the few silver streaks in her hair.

Queenie lifted her bag onto her knees and removed a display box of tarts, which she set on the table. "I didn't bring a plate, but the container opens out like a sewing box. Help yourselves."

"These look good — nice assortment of sizes," Gillan said.

"Yes, a friend suggested a range of sizes might work to prevent waste or seeming greed."

It was one of Mitch's many useful suggestions.

"Your business is going well, then?" Branok sounded interested.

"It's very early days yet, but so far, so good. I've put a brochure in with the tarts. Not trying to sell you any, but I thought you might be interested, since it's down to you that I'm able to expand my activities . . . and indeed, carry them out at all without being thrown out of my home."

"What has Master Porthwellian been doing, exactly?" Branok enquired, ignoring her oblique thanks.

"Nothing bad. He just startled me a bit when the lease agreement popped up and then vanished and reappeared. Now I know what he's doing, it's useful for delivering his tart orders." She explained the system with the Cornfellow pottery tureen which headed Oliver's way each week with a consignment of a dozen mixed tarts.

"The old *coot*, trading for tarts at his age," Gillan said.

"He pays the going rate for them."

"I should hope so."

The kettle boiled and Gillan made and brought the tea.

"I'm glad the housing problem has worked out for you, but you said—implied—something else isn't working so well," Branok said as he selected a Ruby Tuesday tart.

Those were Mitch's favourites, but Queenie couldn't risk thinking about him any more just then.

Gillan considered a little and then took an Emerald Isle.

Queenie wondered vaguely whether one could read personalities or moods in the tarts people chose from a large selection. She remembered Branok had asked a question and she hastened to answer it.

"It's the Caledonian Curse—the manifestation as you call it—giving me gyp."

"Didn't you say that was all in October?"

"It is, usually, but it's getting a head start this year. I think I can avoid insulting customers by arranging everything by remote pick-up for the next few weeks . . . I can probably sort out something with Fiddle-de-Dee, the supermarket, and I've ordered a tart hatch from a local joiner. It should be here verra soon."

"What's that?"

She shrugged. "It didnae exist until I invented it. I needed a kind of wooden stand where I can leave orders for prepaying customers to pick up. It mun be cool and ant-proof and waterproof, but easy to open and close. The man I found to make it drew some sketches and promised to send it before the end of the month, which is quicker than I ever hoped for."

Gillan nodded approval.

"I've put it about that I won't be attending markets during October, but I'm terribly worried about finances." She leaned forward. "Living at The Belfry won't prevent me from buying something unsuitable online or by mail order, you see. Since I don't need to pay rent this month or next — the rent kicks in halfway through November — I hoped you might agree to take charge of my nest egg for a few weeks."

The couple looked taken aback.

"Please. I need it to be with someone I trust, and I need it where I can't access it when Caledonia comes calling, but where I can easily take control again once it recedes. There's no point in tying it up for months at a time, and the interest on term deposits would be negligible. Would you be willing to do that for me?"

Branok and Gillan exchanged glances.

"Your parents might be a more natural choice. It's not that we won't help, but surely, they are the people you trust most," Gillan said.

"I trust them, and I love them, but I have an anti-boomerang agreement with them. Besides, they don't believe in Caledonia Calling. And trying to get someone else to help might be like committing myself to a mental institution on a voluntary basis and then finding out I couldn't sign myself out. I'm *not* crazy, or disturbed, and in general I'm capable of managing my own affairs. Mum and Dad made sure I understood how to handle money, legal obligations, and social situations before they turned me loose." She turned to Branok. "As you said when I came to see you in August, they did the best they could by me."

"I'm sure they did," Gillan said, with more warmth than Queenie had yet heard from her. "Bran and I would do anything for our sons and their families."

"Even back when they were thorough-going pains in the bum," Branok agreed.

"Obviously you're not incapable," Gillan said, reverting to the subject. "The fact that you're making provision for yourself in this way proves that." She reached out for the tart box again, choosing a Strawberry Fool on the Hill.

Queenie wondered if fairies ever put on unwanted weight. Gillan's ruby dress displayed a splendid figure that could have belonged to a woman half her age.

"Will you do it? I can pay whatever fee is usual. I'm not destitute, and I'm not presuming on our relationship, which is not all that close.

"Because of your recommendation to Porthwellian Tredennick I'm saving a nice bit on rent for the first quarter, but I can't afford to fritter away my only proper asset on Scottish holidays."

"We can do it," Branok agreed. His hand hovered over the tart box before he selected a Queen of Hearts. He took a small bite and then he added, "I think the simplest solution is for you to open a new bank account and add one or the other of us — or even both of us — as co-signatories. Transfer the funds to that account, and once it's in, it will need all three of us to take anything out. Then, once the problem mitigates, we can all sign the funds out and you can put them back in your usual account. There are other ways, but that's the simplest."

"You might even get a better-than-usual interest rate on a brand-new account," Gillan said.

"Thank you. Could we do that today?"

"I expect so. Do you want to use your own bank?"

"You'd get a better deal from a new one, but on the other

hand there might be a delay in transferring money between banks when you want to go back to normal," Gillan said.

"My own, I think."

Branok nodded approval. "Whenever you're certain the danger is past, come back to us and we'll all arrange the transfer."

"Could we do it next year too?"

"Can't see why not," Branok said.

Gillan put in, "It would be even simpler next year. We needn't close the account—just leave a small sum in it to avoid extra fees. You could put the money in any time you think it needs protecting from your mani . . . *or* from anyone else."

"Who else?" Queenie asked.

Gillan cleared her throat. "I'm not suggesting you're gullible, my dear, but the best of us can be a little malleable when we acquire a lover. That's why Bran and I, although we have a joint account and trust one another absolutely, also keep a small proportion of our finances separate. Thus, if I want to buy a wholly unnecessary frivolous gift for a delightful grandbaby, Bran need not know and has no right to comment on my folly."

"Or if I chose to acquire a standing order of tarts, Gill would have no say in the matter," Branok murmured. He glanced at the depleted box.

"No," Gillan said. "More than two tarts would be plain greedy."

Branok ostentatiously chose a second Ruby Tuesday.

Queenie watched the byplay with mild amusement, but in the back of her mind she wondered whether Gillan had meant anything particular with her comment about lovers.

I have acquired a lover . . . how could she know? Is she psychic? Or does it show in my face or demeanour?

They finished their morning tea and then walked a couple of blocks to the bank, where Queenie requested the new account.

The manager seemed cautious. "Ms Hart, you do realise that if you have three mandatory signatories there could be a problem if one of you is incapacitated or if you have a falling out. Why do you want to do this?"

Queenie had no intention of telling him about the Caledonian Curse, and she couldn't imagine falling out with the St Ives couple. They had offered her nothing but goodwill, and they didn't associate often enough to quarrel. Gillan's comment on family suggested she felt a connection with Queenie, even though they weren't related by blood. She supposed incapacitation might be a problem, though.

The bank manager explained, "One of my clients had everything tied up so he and his wife were counter signatories to every transaction. He had an accident and was in a coma for five months. Obviously, he was in no condition to sign anything. She had to apply for a court order to release the funds, and it took a long time."

"Couldn't you release the funds to her?"

"No, Ms Hart. If I could, then there would be no point in setting up these double-signatory accounts, would there?"

Branok said, "If you can't see your way to doing this, we'll go to another bank."

The manager said, "That is your prerogative, but any responsible financial institution would give you the same advice."

Queenie said, "Can we set it up for three months at a time? It could be renewed each quarter. That way if something happened to one of us the money would be tied up for a maximum of ninety days before whichever two of us were okay could sign it out."

"Ninety-two, actually," Gillan murmured.

The bank manager frowned. "That would be possible, but it seems unnecessarily complicated. Why not choose a term deposit?"

"Because, wee mannie, we want the money at call . . . so long as the three of us agree, ye ken?" Queenie said.

She felt a flood of lassie haggis rolling her Rs and she clenched her hands to hold it back.

The bank manager looked startled at her change of diction, but he capitulated. "You realise you three will have to be physically present at whatever branch you nominate if you need to make a withdrawal . . . It can't be done over the phone or online."

"Three of us present. That's what I want," Queenie said.

The paperwork was unexpectedly quick, possibly because Branok was a solicitor and so understood the terminology, and within half an hour they were back at the office.

Queenie paused on the threshold of the inner room, looking about.

"What's the matter? Do you need the loo?" Gillan asked.

"No . . . but where's Lady Velvet?"

Chapter Five: The Velvet Explanation

Queenie Hart, Late September, 2021

The other two froze.

Queenie expected them to call for their pet, although there seemed nowhere a medium-sized dog could hide in the office.

The box of tarts was undisturbed on the table.

"She couldn't have slipped out after us, could she?" Queenie ventured. It made her feel cold to think that their beloved dog might have come to harm while they were helping her.

The St Ives exchanged one of their fleeting looks, then Branok said, with an odd heartiness. "I'm sure Lady Velvet is fine."

Queenie went to look behind the couch. "She's not shut in the loo, is she? Or—" She ran out of inspiration.

"She's fine," Branok reiterated.

"How do you know? Where is she?"

"Queenie, you're being exasperating again. Can't you take my word for it?"

Queenie closed her mouth, but she couldn't help glancing about.

Finally, Gillan sighed. "It's all right, Bran. I'll show her. Otherwise she'll be fretting herself to flinders or reporting us to the RSPCA or rethinking her trust in us."

"Show me *what*?"

Gillan sat down on the couch and patted the seat beside her. "Sit here, my dear. Just for a moment."

Queenie sat down.

"Now, don't worry. It's quite okay." Gillan folded her hands in a tinkle of silver. Then she bowed her head as if in prayer. For a second Queenie saw a quiver in the air — then the woman vanished.

Where she'd been sitting, the black spaniel appeared. The dog sniffed the air in the direction of the tarts and then gave Queenie a hopeful look.

Queenie stifled a squeak. She turned to stare accusingly at Branok. "What just happened?"

"We told you Lady Velvet was fine, and as you see — she's fine." He came over and gave the dog a rub on the head. "There, my beauty. Show Cousin Queenie you're okay."

Velvet sniffed the air again and nosed at Queenie's leg. She licked her lips.

"She wants a tart," Branok said.

"Can she —"

"She can, but a whole one mightn't be a good idea. She has a canine digestive system in this form, and she masses a good deal less than I do, so a whole tart might be considered greedy."

Velvet gave an indignant yip.

"All right, just the edge of one. Queenie, will you do the honours?"

Queenie opened the box on the table and broke off a piece of Cheesy Grin. She held it out, and the dog took it gently and ate it.

Branok said, "Now, you probably want to go home and never think of your scary cousins again, eh?"

Gillan popped back into view, neat and elegant in her ruby dress. "Bran, don't be defensive. Queenie's not so chicken-hearted, are you my dear? But do close your mouth. And before you ask, what you saw isn't an illusion or any kind of trick."

"C-conjuring?"

"No. You can't conjure sentient beings. It's a mutie manifestation."

"And a pretty extreme one," Branok said, grinning.

"It runs through some pisky families . . . the Teague line, in my case," Gillan explained.

Queenie got command of her voice. "Do Mum and Dad know about you — her?"

"Of course not," Branok said. His grin grew positively fiendish. "Can you imagine Shane's expression if I told him my wife has an extra self who is a dog? Or if he had Velvet in his lap and suddenly — you get the picture."

Queenie pictured it. "Losh!"

Chapter Six: Shortbread

Queenie Hart, Late September, early October, 2021

As Queenie travelled back to Borrowdale Junction in the train, she felt the Caledonian Curse embracing her with renewed vigour. She scarcely dared to open her mouth to acknowledge greetings from locals when she left the train at the station in case she said something unforgivable to someone she liked.

She saw the mini-bus pull in, and she mounted the steps, mutely offering the fare to the driver. She appreciated his face, but she couldn't recognise it and he gave her no hints.

Someone else occupied her accustomed seat, so she moved to the one behind. Her hands shook as she examined her phone, frightened eyes seeking her *aide-mémoire*.

It didn't help, because she was in no position to see the driver's face from this angle.

She rose to get down at the post office stop, but the driver put out his hand to detain her.

"It's me, Queenie. Stay there until I do a drop-off at Oakengrove, and I'll take you home. I need to talk to you. It's important."

She shook her head. "No' tonight."

She was shaken by the revelations of Gillan's other self, and besides, she had a few more batches of tarts to make and deliver before she went into hibernation mode.

"I can't wait," he said.

It might have been an amorous or flirty comment, but his

expression was almost grim.

Queenie said shortly, "You will ha' to. Come tomorrow after five."

"I can't make it tomorrow. I have to take Ayesha to Mum's and get her settled —"

Hurt stabbed through Queenie. She spat out, "Och, is that so? Yer wee moggy needs her paw held, so *I* wait for her convenience?"

"You said you understood," he said reproachfully.

"I didnae. You *assumed* I did. Fair enough — ye need to look after yon moggy but —"

He sighed, seeming exasperated. "Please Queenie, let me take you home now. I'm afraid I can't stay the night, but —"

"I didnae ask ye to!"

"I need to talk to you, to explain things."

"I just said it's no' convenient. If tomorrow evening won't suit you, come the next day."

"I won't be available then."

"Then neither will I! In fact, if you can't make it tomorrow or the next day, I cannae see ye for a month, full-stop."

"But that's what I'm trying to tell you! I'm tied up for the next two days and I won't be able to —"

"Then it's a guid thing I'm nae' wanting ye!" she snapped.

"Please, Queenie . . . love . . ." He held out his hands in appeal.

"Dinnae ye *loe* me, Mitchell Kingsolver. Go an' *fix* whatever has ye so busy — too busy for me!"

"Just as you like." He withdrew his hands.

Queenie flounced down the steps.

She hastened home to The Belfry. There was a large package leaning against the wall, but she went straight past it and locked herself in.

After twenty minutes or so, the Curse lifted its thrall, and she could think straight again, but she knew it would come back, and soon it would be in full flow.

She had already composed a notation for her website.

She recalled the large package, and so she went out to investigate.

It turned out to be the wooden hatch she'd ordered from the joiner, Xavier Partridge, so she could leave orders for customers to pick up *if I'm away*.

She'd prepaid, and he must have delivered it while she was in Sydney.

She set it up just under The Belfry's outer porch and fastened the provided chain to the metal railing.

The hatch wasn't an ideal solution, but it would be better than insulting or confusing her newly acquired customer base with a tirade of lassie haggis when they came to pick up their tarts.

The Fixer would deliver tarts for you when you can't — you know he would.

The Fixer can go and bile his heid.

Anyway, how likely was it that he'd want to do her any favours after she'd snarled at him?

Tears sprang into her eyes.

How could I have been so horrible to him?

She wished she'd let him have his way. He'd wanted to come home with her. She had orders to make, but she could so easily have prepped her pastry while he got whatever it was off his chest. She could have told him about the Curse. She'd intended to, after all. He *would* understand.

Why did I have to be such a mingin' jinny?

It was too late now.

She'd offended him. Worse, she'd hurt him. Well, he had offended her. He'd tried to push his way into her visit to Branok and then *manage* her.

She had always hated to be managed.

Queenie did her final round of deliveries with Georgiana's tricycle.

It was down to Mitch that she had that handy vehicle too . . . He'd borrowed it from his cousin for her, aye, and made sure it was in top working condition.

Mitch didn't contact her that day and if she saw him, she didn't recognise him.

On Thursday, she holed up in The Belfry and waited for September to tip over into October. She longed to have Mitch in her bed, eating her tarts, sitting in her kitchen, prodding his phone . . . just *there.*

She tried to call him, but his phone was turned off . . . or possibly out of range.

The weekend passed with no visit from Mitch. Not even a call.

Queenie found a silver frame with a small painting of the Loch Ness Monster in it. She had bought it from a junk shop when she was thirteen and interested in all things Scottish.

She undid the back, dispossessed Nessie, and slid in her *aide-mémoire.*

She put it on her nightstand and kissed it with love and remorse.

Och, I love ye . . . an' I'm that sorry . . .

Mitch delivered her supplies from Fiddle-de-Dee on the next Monday. He tapped on the door as usual, but rather than conjure them into the kitchen, he left them neatly stacked next to the new tart hatch.

He was gone before she could persuade herself to the door to — what? Haul him in and ravish him in her bed? Give him another serve of lassie haggis? Sit him down for that long talk? Cuddle him close and sob for forgiveness?

The Caledonian Fugue came over her, and she discovered herself searching *check-me-out* for books of traditional Scottish recipes.

It could have been worse, but she knew she was in trouble when she woke up one morning and realised night-baking was a thing. At some point between retiring at eleven o'clock with *The Fay Companion* and waking at six in the morning to begin the day's orders, she'd evidently found the time to whip up a batch of nine-dozen shortbreads, cunningly stamped with unicorns, thistles and the cross of Saint Andrew.

"Weel noo, what am I to do with you?" she asked in dismay.

She couldn't bin the evidence, because of the waste of butter and carraway seeds, but she sold some of them at a hasty discount from her website blackboard and threw others in as extras with her other orders.

Oliver Porthwellian appreciated his sample, and he promptly added some to his regular order, dooming Queenie to continue to provide something she couldn't remember creating.

She had no idea where the thistle, St Andrew's cross and unicorn stamps had come from or, for that matter, where they'd gone when the night-baking episode was completed.

After the shortbread incident, she locked away the ingredients, but it happened twice more before she accepted that if her conscious mind could lock a cupboard, then her subconscious mind could unlock it. She supposed she could run herself right out of ingredients, but maybe night-shopping was also a thing? She knew it was possible to shop for Scottish terriers and tartan shawls and bagpipe serenades without conscious intention, but what would Duncan Dee make of it if she tripled her order for butter? And what if she added some sheep's stomachs and pluck and extra coarse oatmeal to make up a batch of haggis? What if she went shoplifting as a double-blind to pretend she hadn't done it?

That thought reminded her of the time she called Mitch a randy haggis.

He'd been amused.

The memory depressed her.

He hadn't called.

She'd turned the *aide-mémoire* photograph face down in her bedroom, but after this she removed it from the frame and hid it in the drawer where she kept her winter socks. She opened the one on her phone and sat despairing over it for a full minute.

This was the man who had helped her, obliged her, and who said he loved her, but who had thought so little of their association that he'd put a cat's convenience before hers. He hadn't even bothered to tell her he wasn't human.

His face . . . handsome and smiling . . . unfamiliar.

"Guidbye and guid riddance to ye!" she said as she deleted the photograph.

CHAPTER SEVEN: BATS IN THE BELFRY

Queenie Hart, Mid-October, 2021

Queenie continued with her hermit existence, taking orders online and leaving them in her wooden hatch for pick-up.

Queen of Tarts returns to the market in November, her sign proclaimed.

She slipped similar notes in with the orders.

Partway through October, Duncan Dee delivered an order to The Belfry. Instead of leaving it as Mitch had, he tapped on the door and called out to ask if anything was wrong.

Queenie explained, as coherently as she could, that she was not herself — though not ill with anything communicable.

"Ah, black dog visiting you? Are you okay? Do you need support?"

Tears prickled at his kindness.

"Noo, but—"

"If you have spare tarts I could put them in the deli at Fiddle-de-Dee for a couple of weeks," he offered. He added, hastily, "No commission — you're a good, regular customer and you pay on time."

Queenie tried to swallow the lump in her throat. "That would be gey kind o' ye, laddie."

"Righto — just drop me an email when you have some to spare. And let us know if you need a friend. My wife has a soft shoulder and a good ear. Say the word and she'll come."

After he left, Queenie sat down for a good cry. What on earth was Duncan thinking of her closeting herself and speaking with a cod Scottish accent? She wasn't depressed — she was angry, with her situation, and with herself, and with the Fixer.

She'd thought and hoped a move away from the city would ease the problem of the Caledonian Curse. She supposed it had . . . she was managing without a paying job for the quarter, and she'd gained ideas for expanding the offerings from Queen of Tarts. No one had the faintest objection to her baking at any hour of the day or night. She need not see a soul for weeks at a time.

The loneliness was a blessing and a problem.

She rang Andy, just to hear a voice with whom she could have an unguarded conversation.

"Greet you, Queenie."

"Greet you," she managed. That was one of the salutations mentioned in *The Fay Companion*. As she understood it, she could have responded with *Greet you, master,* but since she and Andy were about the same age and acquainted on first name terms, she could get by with the short form.

"How are you travelling?" Andy asked.

"Och, it's all right, really. I'm a wee bit solitary."

"That's understandable. Not spending up big on Scottish castles or antique plaids?"

She laughed. "Noo—I took your advice about me wee nest egg." She explained the arrangement she'd made.

"Excellent! And since your cousin knows your situation, he and Mistress St Ives will turn a deaf ear to any calls you might make to demand funds in the next few weeks."

"Aye, that they will. Andy, would it be verra ill-mannered of me to tell ye aboot somebody else's manifestation?"

She heard a chair creak as he leaned back, possibly to accommodate Dellion or one of his children in his lap. The office at Porthwellian Tredennick appeared to have an inclusive policy regarding family members . . . or maybe the fay didn't use childcare.

Andy said, "That would depend on whether he, or she, bound you to silence . . .or even simply asked you not to mention it."

"No-o, but she wouldnae ha' shown it me if she hadnae been pushed into a corner."

"I should think you could tell us if you don't identify the person," Andy said.

"Besides, we're dying to know," Dellion said.

Queenie puffed out her cheeks. No doubt Dellion had wound her arm around her husband's neck so she could get close to the phone.

She ached with loneliness.

"I went to see someone, and he had a wee dog in his office." That wasn't accurate, as Lady Velvet could not be fairly described as *wee,* but she didn't want to be too specific.

"His—associate came in, and after a while we three went out together. We were not gone verra long, but then we came back, and the wee dog wasnae there. There wasnae anywhere else the hoondie could ha' been scrooched away, and nae doors ajar.

"I was afraid it had got out, but they werenae fashed. It turned oot—"

She broke off. It sounded too bizarre.

Dellion laughed. "Let me guess. You insisted on looking for the dog and they eventually told you the truth just to keep you from being—"

"Exasperatingly persistent," Andy cut in.

"Weel . . ."

"The *wee hoondie* was a manifestation of one of the people," Dellion stated.

"Which means one or both of them were probably pisky, like us," Andy added.

"You're not a wee dog are ye?" She thought he'd make a charming one . . . maybe an elegant whippet.

45

"No, lovie."

"I'm not either, but it runs through a few pisky lines," Dellion said. She made a sound that Queenie thought might mean she was tapping her fingers to count. "There's the Pendennis line—they throw at least one every generation or so—and then the Teagues . . . and there's an odd case of an old scatterblood priest. Then there's the Camelot line—and the Rosevears and Angoves—oh, and Master Warrener, though *he's* not pisky—"

"That's enough, Dellion," Andy said. "Let's say this kind of mutie manifestation is uncommon, but not unheard of. I know *of* some, but apart from Derry—that is, Master Warrener—I don't know them personally. You might find something in *The Fay Companion* . . . look under M-for-Mutable Fay."

"And if you want to know more, you can ask the person concerned," Dellion said.

"She might nae want to tell me, hen."

"It shouldn't be a problem. Most of us—fay—will tell you whatever you want to know, but you have to *ask us,* specifically. We almost never volunteer it."

"Asking implies that you're prepared to listen with an open mind," Dellion continued. She added, softly, "Some people would rather not know, because it makes them uncomfortable, and that's quite okay. After all, *we* don't expect everyone we meet to tell us whether they are human."

Queenie said nothing. She had a nasty feeling, as if she'd stubbed her soul against a brick wall.

Oliver's cultured voice broke in unexpectedly, "We soon learn not to speak uninvited about our heritage, Miss Hart. Many a fay child has been called a liar or been made to write lines to the tune of *I must not make up fanciful untruths.*"

"Why no' conjure a wee cloddie o' clay at their heids?" Queenie asked.

Dellion laughed. "We don't conjure until we've reached the age of reason, sweet. And by then we've learned to keep our traps shut and *integrate*. We call it *passing*."

Queenie realised she'd already known that from her perusal of her housewarming gift. She felt even more foolish.

"Anyway, the habit of reticence is natural to us," Andy said kindly. "You have some fay ancestry, and it must be quite recent, but the information was so suppressed you can't identify the ancestor or ancestors involved. Whoever it was must have *lived human* or *flown under the radar — passed*."

"Don't feel bad, sweet. We all grab the wrong end of the stick sometimes," Dellion said.

Oliver put in, "My tureen will be with you later today, Miss Hart."

"Is it Sunday already?" she asked in dismay.

"No, but my greedy great-grandad believes in being on the front foot where his tarts are concerned," Dellion said.

Oliver harrumphed.

A child's voice interrupted, asking if *Ganpa* had a *red tartie for me*.

Queenie wasn't experienced with young children, but she had no trouble understanding what the little boy meant.

Oliver must be an indulgent ancestor to the small Tredennick boys . . .

She said a hasty goodbye.

Best get baking. I have tarts to make, and clients to appease.

But instead, she sat at her table, feeling even more bereft. She'd given up hankering after Andy as soon as she'd realised he had a wife, but she *did* envy the couple their cosy dynamic.

We decided if we got to twenty and didn't meet anyone we liked better . . . It sounded bizarre, but Andy and Dellion seemed to think it had worked for them.

She wondered if Dellion counted as a Porthwellian or a Tredennick, or both, in the firm of Porthwellian Tredennick.

She got up at last and, having peeped out to ensure Kirk

Circle was untenanted by anyone she might offend, she went for a walk around the graveyard.

She stopped at *Vicar-ville,* and she had a word with the peaceful stones of the Reverends Purcell, Kirk and Bunting, all of whom had at one time lived in the vanished rectory and worked in her own dear Belfry.

"A great fool I've made o' mysel'. I thought he was being secretive an' all along he was just minding his own business. He didnae deny being a fairy man, he just didnae volunteer it. And I made a fuss and so he tried to make a time to tell me, an' I wouldnae gi' him the chance. At least I think that was what he was trying to do — why could I no' be civil to him, an' let him have his say?"

The bygone vicars said nothing, of course, but she felt no condemnation from them, either.

She returned to The Belfry, and on a whim, she tugged at the wooden loop that fastened the door leading up into the belltower.

She'd done that now and then, but she couldn't believe she'd never followed up on her ambition to explore up there before.

Perhaps she'd not had time, with all the business of buttering metaphorical bread and establishing herself in her new community and then arranging to function in it at arms' length for a month.

It felt oddly like trespassing, to insist on opening a door that was reluctant to give up its secrets, but she assured herself it was fine. The Belfry was hers for three months, and for longer if she behaved herself.

The only things she mustn't do were mess with the structure or make major cosmetic changes.

She'd go up right now and see if the bells were still there. Maybe she could polish them.

The door resisted her initial tug, as it had the first time, and so she had another, more determined go.

There was no visible latch—just the loop of stiff rope. It passed through a round hole in the door, and she assumed it was fastened with a heavy knot on the other side to keep it from pulling back through. She dragged the rope to the side as far as she could and then she leaned in and applied her eye to the narrow gap. She could see little but the dim grey of stone and shadow . . . presumably the steps up to the belltower.

She fetched a torch and switched it on, but most of the beam pooled on the wooden door.

"Och! Auld Scratch fly away wi' ye!" she spat.

She leaned back, hauling on the rope and then she had an odd idea. What if it opened inwards?

She gave the door a hearty shove.

That was no good, so she kicked it. Then she hammered on it with her fists. She was aware that her anger had little to do with the door which, for all she knew, was nailed up for safety, and after a while, she stopped.

Nae guid bruisin' my hands and toes.

In the quiet that followed her assault on the door, she heard a sound. It was a scratching, flapping, squeaking sound.

Queenie froze.

There's something behind this door.

She scooted away, back to her kitchen, where she got to work, but every so often, she held her breath and closed her eyes, listening for the tell-tale sounds.

Scritch-scritch . . . rustle-whiffle . . . and was that the faintest of squeaks?

She turned on some bagpipe music to drown the sounds, and almost convinced herself that she'd imagined them.

Though . . . hadn't she heard the occasional rustle and put it down to the corbies, the black-clad birds that liked to perch on the belltower?

Maybe it was them?

She went back to the door, but the sounds seemed much closer than before.

She went to bed on the mezzanine floor, only to wake to a renewed set of rustlings and flutterings.

There must be a wee bird in there.

It didn't sound very wee.

Maybe it really was one of the crows or ravens she heard cawing in the dark trees. It might be trapped.

I ought to see. We trapped folk should stand together.

She pictured herself creeping up to the door with an axe and hacking the door down.

Noo, a hacksaw would make less noise . . .

Though who the sound of her chopping was going to disturb was beyond her. There was no one at Kirk Circle but herself, the birds, and the folk who slept in the graveyard.

She lay in bed swithering with indecision.

Would hacksawing her way through the belfry door count as a *structural change*? She didn't want to get on Oliver's bad side. He was a gentleman of the old school, but she knew he could be cutting at times. If he laid into her with his sharp tongue, she might call him something so unforgiveable that he'd come personally to throw her out of The Belfry. Or have Andy do it.

He would no' do that to me.

She slipped on the jacket she'd been wearing earlier and returned to the narthex for another assault on the door.

She banged with her fist. "Quiet up there, beasties!"

The sounds ceased, but when she returned to bed, they began again.

She couldn't sleep with this going on.

Her skin crept.

I'm alone.

Queenie went back to the narthex yet again and wrestled with her desire to find out who or what was in the belltower and, if possible, to eject it.

Rats. Birds. Ghoulies. Bats. Bogles. Someone's manifest . . .
She shivered.

Gillan St Ives' manifestation, Lady Velvet, was a pleasant if reserved creature, but who knew what other fay harboured in their psyches, ready to make over their bodies at will?

Gillan and Branok had *assured* her manifestations weren't harmful, except—she was sure there had been an exception, but they hadn't spelled it out.

No wonder the fay who *lived human* didn't tell random people who and what they were as a matter of course. They were probably afraid of stirring up a modern-day Salem-witch-hunt-revisited.

A woman who turns into a dog . . . and a black *dog at that!*

She visualised what an ill-informed, ill-intentioned and undisciplined mob might want to do with Gillan if they discovered what she was. She cringed.

And wha' about my ain sel'?

At least her lassie haggis Scotchwoman didn't change her appearance . . . as far as she knew. If she could manage to keep her mouth shut and not to slip into bizarre or confrontational behaviour, then she, like most of the fay, could fly under the radar.

Lassie Haggis . . . That's wha I'll name her.

Her unease about her situation grew, ballooning into fear.

Maybe the former tenants had left The Belfry for reasons *other* than Oliver's conjuring habit.

She'd dismissed the spookiness Branok asked about much too lightly.

She could call Porthwellian Tredennick in the morning, and interrogate Oliver—if she dared—but how was she to get through the night? She certainly couldn't ring them now. Maybe they lived at the offices, or had their offices where they lived, but no couple with little children and an almost antique senior partner would welcome a midnight telephone call from her. It would startle them, and probably wake the

51

children. Besides, what could *they* do? They were a thousand kilometres away!

Her misery grew.

Finally, with a guilty glance at the witching hour displayed on the clock that hung above the locked door, she took her phone out of her jacket pocket, and keyed in a familiar number as fast as she could.

The phone rang distantly, four times.

The fifth ring was interrupted by a soft voice. "Hello."

"Don't ye ever sleep, ye skelpit erse?" she demanded, as the Curse tore through her resolve to be conciliatory.

"Sometimes I sleep a lot, but not so much lately, dearie."

There was something odd about his voice.

"Mitch? Is that you?"

"What's wrong, Queenie? I assume something is, as you're ringing this phone at this hour."

"I'm in a wee fix."

"Another one?"

"Aye, ye cleckity tawse — else I'd no' hae been driven to call ye."

"Was it so difficult to call?"

Queenie felt a surge of dismay at his tone. He sounded altogether unlike himself . . . well, she supposed she *had* woken him and possibly annoyed Ayesha.

She pictured a sleek grey cat yawning with her fishbone-white fangs revealed and peering about with slitted eyes for the woman who had disturbed her repose.

She clutched at what she thought of as her *right mind* and then she said, quietly, "Ye — you said you'd come if I called. I was angry and out of order — I should have said yes — Mitch, I'm so *sorry*."

"I'll come now — but first, can you tell me the manner of your current fix?"

Queenie said mournfully, "Aye, I hae bats in ma belfry."

CHAPTER EIGHT: JAMES STUART REDUX

Queenie Hart, Mid October, 2021

Queenie thought she heard a catch of his breath.

"Don't ye laugh at me, wee mannie, or I'll pu' a hex in yer sporran."

"Could you?" he asked.

"Noo," she admitted. She squeezed her fingernails into her left palm. "I'm sorry I insulted you. I'm no' — not — in my heid sometimes."

"But you really do have bats in your belfry? Literal bats?"

"I dinnae ken . . . but there's some beastie in there keepin' me from ma rest."

"I know the feeling," he said.

"Ye'll come to me?"

"Aye, I'll come right over. Wait for me, dearie."

He ended the call.

Queenie remained where she was, with her arms wrapped around her knees.

Wait for me. She was in no position to do anything else.

The scratching and fluttering continued, but she was sure it would stop the instant she heard Ethel out there on the gravel. That was the way things happened.

He'd think she'd made it up, just to annoy him. Just to get him to come.

She'd see that in his face . . . which she still couldn't picture . . . and Lassie Haggis would fly at him with a flood of invective.

She felt for her phone, to ask him not to come.

Scritch-squeak

Tyres sounded outside and stopped.

After a few seconds, the phone rang in her hand.

"Aye?"

"Queenie, it's me."

"Who else would it be?"

"That's rather the point," he said. "Listen, Queenie, dearest, I need you to do something for me . . . or rather to *not* do something. Will you promise?"

"I cannae look at my *aide-mémoire*," she said in a trembling voice.

"Good. I was going to ask you not to. Just take it on trust that this is me."

"Who else—"

"Let's not do that again. Will you let me in, dearie?"

"Let yerself in, *fix-it pixie*. Ye've done it before," she said.

"Would you rather I went away?"

"Noo—no, please." She felt near to tears with the mix of emotions. "Conjure yourself in."

"I can't do that if I have no right to enter."

"I gie ye the right."

"Good. Thank you, my dearest."

His voice sounded relieved, but it still sounded odd. Was it really Mitch out there? She yearned to check her *aide-mémoire,* but she'd deleted the one on the phone and the other was up in her sock drawer. Besides, he'd asked her not to.

The door swung open, and she saw him framed against the dark. He was facing her squarely, a stranger—yet, not quite . . .

Queenie released her grip on her knees and scuttled backwards as fast as she could, blushing fiercely.

The man in front of her sighed. "Ah, *lord.* You can see my face—see me as I am."

"Aye," she said in a strangled voice.

He held out both hands to her and she cringed.

"Queenie, it's all right. It's *me.*"

She shook her head. "It's not. I wouldnae know ye, I never can, and I do!"

"It's me."

She shook her head. "I see ye as plain as the nose on yer mug, James Stuart. Where's Mitch?"

He passed a hand around the back of his neck, and briefly tugged at his tied-back hair. "Queenie, dearie, could we go into the kitchen and talk?"

"Talk, is it!"

"Please?"

The Glasgow accent was strong, but he spoke with a standard dialect. His loch-grey eyes looked sad, and his auburn hair complemented a pale Celt's complexion.

After a bit, she nodded. She'd been strongly attracted to James Stuart on their one encounter a year earlier on Circular Quay — so much that she'd sought him for months afterwards.

He'd liked her, too, but she'd been properly dressed then. Now she was hunched up in a plaid jacket pulled over the outsized T-shirt and loose-legged knickers she'd worn to bed. Her feet were bare.

He, on the other hand, wore an argyle sweater in soft grey and blue tones over muted cords and soft leather brogues. It was exactly the way she remembered him from the year before.

She got up as gracefully as she could. "The kitchen's through there," she said carefully, indicating the door in the partition that divided the long body of the former church. "I'll go an' dress mysel'."

"Not on my account."

"Noo, bampot! On mine."

She hurried up to the mezzanine floor and pulled on some leggings. And then she scrabbled in her sock drawer and drew out the crumpled *aide-mémoire* – the photograph Mitch had given her so that she could identify him after he'd left her breakfast.

She straightened it as well as she could and then, with no excuse to linger, she went reluctantly to her kitchen.

James had got the jug on to boil, but he was standing in the middle of the room, with his hands thrust into his pockets. He looked at her warily.

"Still recognise me?"

She nodded. "We met about a year ago down at Circular Quay. You pointed out I had flour on my shirt, and you invited me for a drink."

"And you turned me down."

"Aye. Yes. I did. I wanted to go wi' ye, but I was sure I'd make a walloper o' mysel' . . . I'd already –"

She broke off.

He smiled and reminded her. "You called me a *mingin' jimmy* and threatened to put some of my bits in a jar and make the rest into a haggis. It was the most entertaining and emphatic putdown I'd ever experienced."

"Aye, that sounds about the way o' it," she agreed sadly.

"You thought I'd insulted you with my well-meant gesture at your chest."

She nodded.

"So you insulted me right back."

The jug bubbled.

James turned to take down two cups. "Appropriate for a place like this," he said.

"Ye what?"

"The pattern on these cups."

She stared at him uncomprehendingly.

He handed her one. "Bats for the belfry," he added.

Queenie looked at the cup, at the lacy black pattern she'd taken for leaves. It was so obvious now she couldn't work out why she hadn't seen it before. The floating black shapes were tiny bats, tossed by an invisible wind.

James spooned tealeaves into the matching bat-patterned teapot, which she had never used, and poured the bubbling water over it. "Best let it steep," he said.

Queenie said, accusingly, "I always use teabags."

"I know. I happen to prefer leaf tea, so I—brought some over for you. I hope you don't mind."

He leaned against the granite counter looking at her with a mix of exasperation and affection.

"Queenie Hart, Queen of Tarts, queen o' my heart, however did we let it come to this? Made a right muckle mess o' it, between us."

Queenie shook her head. It was embarrassing standing reminiscing in her kitchen with a young man she'd met just once before. He looked as neat as a bandbox, as they said in the historical romances her mother Liberty descried but which Queenie had always loved.

She, on the other hand, looked like something the cat dragged in and didn't fancy. If she'd had a cat.

Mitch was the one with the cat. Ayesha, the ice queen.

"What?" he asked.

"Are you real? Or a—a—seeming? Imagination—a dream?"

"I'm real. Take my hand."

She put one hand in his and he squeezed gently.

"What's that you're clutching?"

He unfolded the fingers of her other hand and removed the creased photograph from her grasp.

"I asked you not to look at this."

"As if ye've the right!" she blurted.

"I haven't, of course. I don't have rights. My kind can't. It was for your sake, really, but—" He looked down at the picture. "This is no way to treat a gift from an admirer. Whatever have you been doing with it?"

She said, shamefacedly, "It's been in my sock drawer, as if it's anything to do wi' you. It's no from an admirer, but from a dear friend, to recall his face to me."

She backed away and sat down at the small table. "I called him and asked him to come. He promised he'd come. I needed him to come. *I wanted* him. So why are *you* here?"

"Now you sound more like the Queenie I know. I'll pour our tea and then we'll sort things out, I promise. Strong?"

"Yes. If it's good tea."

"It is. My mother grows it." He turned and poured dark amber liquid into the cups which he set on the table. He opened a crock on the bench and raised his brows. "Shortbread! May I?"

"Help yersel'."

He brought the crock to the table, and he sat down opposite her, dropping the photograph — her precious *aide-mémoire* — casually on the table.

"Shall we try to untangle this mess, Queenie?"

"Aye, but first — where is Mitch?"

He bit his lip. "I could be provokingly mysterious and say *Mitch is here*, but it's more accurate to say Mitch — the Mitchell Kingsolver whose face you can never remember — is unavailable right now."

"He said he'd come to me."

"He's not just unavailable to you, my lovely. He's unavailable, full stop. He's my other self, you see."

Queenie felt as if her eyes were going dry and she had to blink.

I've been here before.

She felt the aromatic vapour from the tea bathing her face, curing the dry air. She breathed it in, grateful for the distraction.

She said, carefully, "I know someone with an extreme manifestation. She's a pisky woman — "

"Pisky miss or pisky minx is the usual term," he corrected.

"Wheesht! Let me hae ma say."

"I beg your pardon."

"This *pisky minx* is also a black spaniel."

His face lit with an unholy grin. "I'd give a guinea to see that!"

She frowned at him. "I did see that. I tried to pat that. And now I see *you, ye sleekit fandan.*"

"That's a wee bit harsh," James said.

"So — yon wee mannie Mitch is yer spaniel bitch!"

James stopped smiling. He pushed back his chair and he got to his feet. A pink patch flamed in each cheek and his grey eyes turned stormy. "If you're trying to be insulting, at least have your facts right. You're implying Mitchell Kingsolver is my manifestation self — " He broke off, leaning forwards and raising a dark auburn brow at her.

"Aye, tha's what I am implying. It's what ye *said.*"

"Then you're wrong, and it's not. And before you gallop off on some other terrible glawket tangent, you've got it arse-aboot, thou rankety she-baw."

What?

"Mitchell Kingsolver is, much as it hurts my consequence to admit it, my main man self. He gets to gang aboot bedding the Queen o' Tarts to his heart's content and his wee willy's satisfaction, squeezing her sweet arse, kissing her titties, while I — " he slapped his broad, diamond-paned chest — "got brushed off and turned down on the quay for my trouble. You're *mine*, Queenie Hart! My lassie and my love! *I saw you first.*"

Chapter Nine: Explanations

Queenie Hart, October, 2021

Queenie gaped at the beautiful Glaswegian throwing a hissy fit in her kitchen. It was enough to shock the Caledonian Curse right out of her psyche for a few seconds, at least.

She had no desire to be loomed at, so she scrambled out of her chair and put her hands on her hips. "What the hell are you talking about?"

"I did! I saw you at the quay! You were beautiful, and generous, and kind. You were in distress, but you gave away your wish, and turned it back to me—and when I came to claim you—"

"Stop! Stop that before I dump my tea over your havering heid and kick yer glacket arse oot of ma kitchen!"

He stopped, breathing hard.

Queenie said, "*What* a mawkish display of self-pity. What the *crumpet* is wrong with you, mun? Claim me indeed! Wheesht mun! How *dare* you!"

He subsided into his chair.

Queenie sat down and put her head in her hands. She wanted to telephone Andy or Branok or Mitch to ask them please to come and sort out this Scottish madman in her kitchen. Maybe Gillan would be a better choice. Lady Velvet could bite his arse. She'd do it with grave precision, and Queenie hoped it would *hurt*.

She fished in her pocket, and she woke her phone with a

stab of her finger.

Then, slowly, she put it away.

Queenie, you have got to stop relying on other folk to get you out of messes.

She pulled herself together. No, she *hauled* herself together, breathing deeply. "James, let me get this straight. I think you're saying *you* were the living statue down at the quay last year. You had a green painted face, and you gave me a wish on a scrap of tartan. Right? No, don't you dare start sputtering again. Just nod or shake your head, once."

He nodded.

"And I'm supposing that since Mitch is a fairy man — a fix-it pixie — you are one too?"

He made no move.

"Okay, we're no' playing charades here. Tell me."

He clasped his hands in front of him, white knuckled. "Aye, I'm a fairy man, although we use the term fay. But I'm not a fix-it pixie. I'm a braw braeside laddie."

Queenie nodded. She'd read about those in Volume 1 of *Orders of the Fay.*

Braesiders were fay aligned to Scotland. The men were laddies from birth to death, and the women were lassies. She'd wanted to meet one, and now she had.

Weel, that explains why I wanted to bring him hame. Just the cup o' tea for Lassie Haggis.

She said, "That must be awkward for you."

"Your situation is clearly awkward for you," he countered. "Whatever that situation may be."

"It is verra awkward, but you're a complete and separate other person. I'm always me — even though I do and say bizarre things in October."

"I'm not quite a separate person," he said dryly. He got up again, and he took a quick turn around the kitchen. "I remember what *he* does — what he thinks and experiences. But I don't share his imperative to *fix* things." He returned to face her, spreading his hands. "Not a fix-it pixie, you see. Not even a pixie."

"Just as jealous as one though," she said.

He hunched his broad shoulders. "Can you blame me, dearie? I had such a short time to be with you, that day. You gave me the wish and I loved you for it and then—you ran away from me."

"I tried to find you though. In November, when the Caledonian Curse lifted, I hung around the quay, embarrassing mysel' and making others uneasy, trying to find ye."

"I was well gone by then."

"Yes, and after a while, I met Mitch instead."

"And you gave him *my* tarts," he growled.

Queenie threw up her hands. She *had* given a free sample courtesy card to the living statue and then she'd run away from James—or rather, from herself—and then Mitch had claimed the sample tarts and eaten them with unmistakable relish on the day of her move to The Belfry. It was all too much for her.

"Technically, I didn't *give* them to him."

"You allowed him to take them, the mèirleach pastraidh!"

"I loe' weel to see a mun eat," Queenie flashed. "It gets me gey hot in the coochie." She heard herself too late, and she clapped both hands over her mouth, staring at him with horrified eyes.

James's eyebrows went up and his eyes widened ominously. He took a stride towards her and Queenie, not wanting to cringe, got slowly out of her seat and stepped away. She held up her hands, palms out.

"Please—"

"I'm not going to hurt you."

"If I thought ye were, I'd gie ye a kick in the baws!"

"Settle down. I'm not going to—"

"Then *sit down.* Stop stalking aboot like some lang-leggedy beastie — "

He sat down.

Queenie came back to the table. She pulled her jacket around her shoulders, and she took several deep breaths, supressing Caledonia as hard as she could.

In that inappropriate moment, she was ridiculously aware of her dishevelled state. *He*, on the other hand, looked as if he'd just stepped out of a men's fashion catalogue, circa 1920s. He should be leaning on a mantelpiece, beaming at a perky wife and holding a pipe negligently in one hand.

He was beautiful — and exasperated.

She said, "Is there any way I can talk to Mitch right now?"

"No." He scowled at her, with resentment radiating from him like heat from a compost heap in summer.

"Really no way, or are you just being Scottish and obstructive?"

"I'm not Scottish."

She waved her hand to push this away.

He harrumphed and then he said, "Really no way, lassie." He added, with surprising gentleness, "I would let you if it were in my power."

"But you remember being him . . . so can you explain why he didn't tell me what he was?"

"Not exactly, because he doesn't think the way I do. I wouldn't put up with being used as a convenience by that blasted she-cat of his — she hates me. Don't look like that! The ice queen is perfectly safe. Our mother is looking after her — she always does when I'm in the ascendent. Ayesha can't be doing with me any more than I can be doing with her, and I have the claw-marks to prove it. He takes her to Mum a day or so before I step up, and he stays with her to get her settled. Once — just *once* — he left it too late. The result wasn't pretty."

He breathed in deeply and continued with less anger, "As for disclosing to you, I expect he was thinking along the lines that telling you we're fay wasn't enough . . . because of our differences. He knew I was coming back, and he couldn't bring himself to tell you. He wanted you to himself."

He stopped and frowned and then he added, half-reluctantly, "He did *intend* to talk things out with you. He knew he had to explain about me because I *would* manifest. He left it too late, just as he did the time with Ayesha."

"He's had weeks to tell me."

"Weeks to woo you," he said sourly.

"Oh, was *that* what he was doing?"

"What else would you call it? Helping you out, *whistle and I'll come to ye, my lassie* . . . oh, he knows his Rabbie Burns, just as I do. *I'll always come to you.* What else was *that* but a wooing?"

"I thought it was because he wanted to fix things," Queenie said. "He kept saying that."

"He does! But he wanted to come to you, the sleekit dafty. He wanted to soak in every moment with you . . . hold you in his arms forever."

"He should have told me," Queenie said.

"He should. Only you didn't make it easy, blowing hot and cold. What *is* it with you and the insults and October, and all that outlandish gabble? You mentioned a curse?"

"I thought you knew about that."

He shrugged. "How could I? *He* knows there's something about October that bothers you, but you never told either of us exactly what it is."

So I didn't.

Queenie thought back. She'd explained herself to Branok and Gillan, and to Andy and Dellion—and Oliver undoubtedly knew—but other than that, she hadn't sat down and explained to *anyone*. Not after her parents, the people who loved her and who should have always had her back, had so patently disbelieved her.

She said, "I thought you—and he—knew because you both

accepted the lassie haggis . . . what did you think it was?"

His shoulders rose again. "He—and I—knew there was something at work inside your beautiful head, but who is he to pry? As I believe he once told you, it takes one to know one."

"I see. If I tell you about it, will he know too?"

"Yes. If he's paying attention."

"And will he get all upset and hurt and offended because I told *you* rather than *him*?"

He shrugged.

She wished he wouldn't do that.

"Will he?" she snapped.

"I can't tell you. And at this moment, I don't care. *He* had weeks to ask you, and to tell you, as you said."

"Okay—and before you get smug, I'm telling you only because you're here. I did mean to tell him. But, like him, I didn't want to spoil things. And then in the end the bluidy Curse came in early and I couldnae think straight or find a civil tongue in ma heid—" She caught herself up.

"Take a breath if you need one, dearie," he said gently.

He sounded so like Mitch in that moment that Queenie could almost think it was her lovely Fixer before her . . . and even yet she couldn't picture his face. She groped in her pocket, but she'd deleted the photo and the printed *aide-mémoire* lay face down on the table where he'd dropped it, and she didn't quite dare to reach for it.

She closed her eyes to shut out temptation.

Then she leaned back, and she took a sip of her cooling tea.

She was unexpectedly thirsty, so she drained the cup. "Might I have another one?"

"It's your kitchen, dearie."

Dearie. That was all James. Mitch never called her that.

"And your tea," she pointed out.

He got up to reboil the jug, emptied the teapot and began

the whole ritual again.

Queenie slowly reached for her *aide-mémoire* and transferred it to her lap. She looked down at it.

A handsome, smiling olive-skinned face looked back at her, slightly bent and dog-eared from being jammed into her sock drawer. The name, *Mitchell Kingsolver*, was scrawled across the green shirt in her handwriting. She stared at the face of the man who had been kind, and loving and, in the end, maddening in his insistence that he must talk to her *now* . . .

She looked up at James, pale-skinned, with just a hint of fresh colour in his cheeks, grey-eyed and with hair in that dark, foxy auburn, tied back.

My perfect laddie.

This time, he brought the pot to the table and set it between them.

"Tell me, love," he said, sitting down across from her again. "I'll pour the tea when it's steeped."

If he noticed she'd fielded the photograph again, he didn't mention it.

Queenie glanced down.

This is for you, Mitchell Kingsolver. It's what I wish I had told you and what I should have told you.

She said, "So this is Queenie Maeve Hart one-oh-one for both of you."

She blew out her cheeks, and she began.

CHAPTER TEN: IN THE BEGINNING

Queenie Hart, Mid-October, 2021

"In the beginning, when I was about thirteen, we had a Halloween unit at school."

Queenie wondered if James knew about school, but now wasn't the time to start insulting him by assuming he was ignorant. "It was art and literature, history and RS and—oh, they managed to work it into just about every point in the curriculum. Halloween isn't much of a *thing* in Australia. Well, it wasn't back then. I was really interested in it, though. I especially loved the *lang-legged beasties* poem. We did some Robbie Burns . . ."

He was definitely familiar with that poet, anyhow. He'd said so.

"I turned out to be *gey guid* at reading in dialect. I could sight read that *Whistle and I'll Come to Ye* song. I even sight-read some of the mediaeval texts our literature teacher brought to show us . . . they were facsimiles of course, but no one else could get more than a word or two into them."

She shrugged. "For about five minutes the school thought I was *gifted*, but Dad and Mum soon put them right about that."

He raised his brows. "Are ye no'?"

She smiled at his trip into dialect, and she wondered briefly if that was the way he wanted to speak, and if his mainstream vernacular was an affectation. Or was it the other way around?

"I'm glad they did! I'm *not* gifted. My IQ is normal."

"I doubt that, bonnie lassie."

"It is! Well, maybe a few points north of absolute average, but I'm certainly not unusual."

His eyebrows shot up even higher.

"Not in IQ, anyway," she specified. "If I'd been pushed into extension programs, I'd have been miserable. I decided to think it was just a weird flash in the pan—especially at Christmas, when my best friend got me to do my party piece for a Scots relative whose speciality was linguistics and the early modern period. I stumbled through the sample text—better than my friend, but not fluent. My friend was mortified. The expert relative was . . ."

"Condescending?" he prompted.

"Kind." She sighed. "The next year, we were putting up bats and cats and things in the library display when I found the texts the teacher had brought in the box with the decorations—and I could read them again. I was silly enough to show off to Maddison—my friend—and after that we weren't best friends anymore." The memory of what Maddison had said still scorched her, after a decade.

She put away the memory and continued. "And then my other friends at school started saying I was talking funny, and I got into trouble for being impolite to a teacher. I think I called her a sleekit baw-cat. Mum thought I was being disruptive, and cheeky—Dad said it was just a phase—but it got worse. I didn't know what was wrong with me—and neither did Mum and Dad. After they realised I couldn't help it, they took me to various people to try to find out. One diagnosis suggested Asperger's and another that I was a savant. Some said it was a phase and I'd get over it if less attention was paid to it. One person even suggested demonic possession."

"I'm sure that went down well," he said.

"Not very. No. Mum called him a few choice names . . . and

not in lassie haggis. Her command of the English language is better than mine and she could use it to strip paint when she's angry.

"Because the condition was only apparent in October, none of the ideas seemed to fit the facts. I was still interested in Scottish folklore and such, although I stopped talking about it in self-defence. That's when I started calling it the Caledonian Curse."

"It doesn't seem to be afflicting you now," he observed.

"No, and that's odd, because it's the witching month and usually stress makes it worse. Even outside October it occasionally sneaks up on me when I'm rattled. That's one reason I moved up here."

"Only one reason?"

"I had problems with my landlady and with work—you know all this, or rather, Mitch does."

"Yes, but I thought maybe there was another reason unconnected with those."

"If you must know, meeting you at the quay was the last straw—I mean *not* meeting you. For months I kept going back there to look for you. It upset the O-Quay Café folk and I finally realised I was cultivating an unhealthy obsession. I do have obsessive tendencies. When I latch onto something I like, I *will* try to—have it."

He nodded. His fine-featured face looked—smug.

"Wha' are ye gloating aboot, neepheid?" Queenie snapped.

"I was feeling pleased that you did want me." James seemed unabashed at being caught out and taken up. He added, "I'm pleased to know that I hadn't spoiled my chances to impress you . . . and wasted your wish."

Queenie didn't retort that wishes had no validity because, according to *The Fay Companion,* they did. Not every wish came true, but the right one, made in the hearing of the right fay ears, easily might.

"I cannae even recall what I said," she said mendaciously.

"I can, though I'll paraphrase . . . You dropped me the most ravishing curtsy, giving me a grand view of the canyon of paradise, slightly dusted with flour. You wished me good fortune and sweet dreams at night, and you asked that luck and love should attend me always. It sounded a good deal more poetic than that when you said it."

"It sounds mish-mashy mimsy-wamsy to me."

"Not at all. It's a kind and generous wish—and it offered me love—something I could never have hoped for otherwise."

"Why could ye not?" she said, frowning. She was annoyed with him, but he was beautiful, and she had been drawn to him when they first met. She still was. He had gey beautiful eyes, an' that braw arse—

She pulled herself up as Caledonia-on-my-mind sought to drown her in lust and desire. She hadn't even realised she'd noticed his arse. It must have been when he turned to make the tea.

And that reminded her. She reached for the steaming pot and poured herself a cupful. Then she absently reached for his cup and filled that too.

She replaced the pot between them just as he reached out for his cup—and took hers instead.

Ye sleekit—

James said, "Why couldn't I hope for love? Isn't that obvious?"

Because ye're a sleekit baw—

He went on, "I exist for one month out of twelve. How can love ever attend me, as you expressed it, except in the general family sense of the word? Mum loves me dearly . . . she calls me her *braw October laddie*, but that's understandable. I'm the only one in the family who looks like her. She's a fine figure of a lassie, is Danna Kingsolver."

Queenie bit her lip in indecision. She saw his problem. She

had eleven unencumbered months every year but still she couldn't keep boyfriends for long. Quite aside from her desire to watch them eat, they found her abrupt left turn into Caledonian Curse linguistic territory a bridge too far.

"We're a fine pair, laddie," she said. "But still, ye're real — solid — a person." She tried for a slight change of focus. "How did you choose your name? Your mother is Danna Kingsolver and your dad — "

"Beaman . . . and yes, it does have to do with bees." He laughed. "As for *my* name, it didn't come about the way your parents chose yours, Queenie Mary Victoria Adelaide Elizabeth Hart. Which one was deemed your middle name, by the way? Or do you use them all?"

"Maeve, remember? It's the only name they could come up with that used all the initials . . . Mum's heavily into wordplay, and she was out of all reason pleased with that name."

"M for Mary, A for Adelaide, E for Elizabeth and V for Victoria. But it has an extra E," he commented.

"Aye, and the extra E is the one missing from *heart* in the spelling of our last name. *Perfect*, Mum says. I asked why they didn't choose it for my first name, but Mum says she didn't think of it until too late. Dad was already calling me Queenie and he wasn't going to budge."

"Would you rather be a Maeve?" he asked.

"On balance . . . no. Queenie is an odd name. It's never been especially popular, but it *is* a real name from an Old English word. But Maeve is Irish, and that doesn't feel right to me. I'm happy to have it in my name, but it isn't *me*." She sipped her tea, enjoying the rich scent. He was right. It was *much* nicer than the generic teabags she bought. "I see now how Mitch came to know the story of my first name. I knew I hadn't told him."

"You told *me*."

She waved a hand in dismissal. "How *did* you choose your

own name, if your parents didn't?"

"Technically, I didn't *choose* it. Not from scratch. Mani folk like me don't — exist, develop, wake — however you like to put it — until around the time the main personality hits puberty. I have no memories of early childhood. My memories of *his* life start from when he was twelve or so, but I didn't really get my autonomy until I'd been around for two years. By then, it was obvious I was going to be a permanent entity and not just a hormonal aberration or offshoot of the main personality. Once my parents understood I was *me,* and that they'd be dealing with me for a month of every year from then on, they asked what I wanted to be called. I didn't know. I was *me* — the laddie. I might have used that — a lot of mani-folk do go by descriptives — but my mother, Danna, said I was as much her son as *he* was, and she suggested I might like the two middle names *he* doesn't use — and that I could choose the order."

"Stuart James or James Stuart."

He flashed her a grin. "Aye, it was lucky either would do as a surname. I chose to leave the order as it was. Stuart was Mum's name before she wed with Dad, and James is the male form of Mum's second name, which is Jamesina."

"So he's Mitchell James Stuart Kingsolver."

"Yes, but he uses the *JS* as initials. If *I* needed middle names, which I don't, I'd have *MK.*" He added, after a moment, "If it were not for the connection with Mum, I'd have asked for a separate name, but I wanted to honour her. I love Dad, but he already had *his* son-in-his-own-image."

"Your parents are a wee bit more understanding than my ain," Queenie said. She added, "To be fair, it would be a wee bitty easier if I *looked* different when Lassie Haggis is aboot. They'd hae to believe in her then."

They looked at one another ruefully.

"I'd find it easier if I looked like *him,* although I don't want to," James said.

Then Queenie said, "When I called Mitch tonight, you answered his phone. Why?"

"Well, *he* couldn't." He cleared his throat. "Generally, I don't answer the Fixer phone. After a few rings, it goes to message bank where the caller is informed that the Fixer will be available on November the second. I just keep it by me in case Danna and Beaman or the sistren call it by mistake. They're not very used to phones. I do drive the bus, and sometimes do deliveries for Fiddle-de-Dee, but *he* has another phone for that."

"Don't folk notice the difference?" Queenie pushed the shortbread crock his way. She was hungry, but she didn't care to eat alone.

James took a piece, and he examined it before taking a bite.

"You could have tarts if you'd rather," she said.

James slid her a glance, chewing. "*He* loves the tarts."

"You've never even tried one, sheepheid!" she said, nettled.

"You gave *him* the ones you promised me. But I like this. It's as good as Granny Elspeth's recipe." He took another bite.

Queenie repeated her question. "Don't folk notice when *you* drive the bus instead of Mitch? Do you even have a licence?"

"What do *you* think?"

"I expect they do. You don't look anything like him."

"How do you know?" he challenged. "You can't remember his face."

"I have this." She held up the *aide-mémoire* from her lap. "So, do they?"

He shrugged. "I'm his official sub. I think they believe I'm his Scottish cousin or a half-brother or something."

"Why do you sub for him, since you don't like him?"

"Did I say I didn't like him?"

"Let's just say you implied it."

He scowled and then he nodded reluctantly. "He doesn't want to lose the bus run or the deliveries through being unavailable for a month."

"So, you help him out from the goodness of your heart."

"I do not. But . . . I can't exactly hold down a normal job. By the time I applied and got fairly started, I'd be gone. Therefore, we share *his* work."

"You don't deal with the Fixer business though."

"How can I? I'm not a fix-it pixie. He doesn't advertise in October, and his website says he's *unavailable*, just the same as his phone."

Just like my website and blog.

Queenie contemplated him for a while. He was extraordinarily attractive. She'd loved the friendly, eager, adaptable person she'd met back on Circular Quay. This version was cross and complex, but then, he had a right. She couldn't forget his face when he'd told her mani folk such as him had no rights.

She drained her tea. Then she glanced at the kitchen clock.

It was an hour and a half past midnight. She said, "James, I'm sorry I called you out tonight."

He reached for another piece of shortbread. "I'm not. I was longing to see you again."

"Why didn't you, then? You've been around for a couple of weeks. You know where I live."

"I delivered some things for you, but you didn't answer your door. I came here twice. Duncan got worried when I said I hadn't seen you, and he did the next delivery himself."

"I see. I try to keep well away from folk when Caledonia is calling."

"Then why were you at the quay that time?"

She explained, briefly, about the almost-purchased round trip to Edinburgh that had driven her to run away from her phone and laptop.

"I was terrified I'd lose my nest egg, so I just had to get

away from temptation. Anyway, I really am sorry to disturb you for nothing, so late at night."

"Bats in the belfry isn't nothing."

"No." She shivered, remembering the original reason — one of them — that she'd called the Fixer line. "But *you* can't help me with that. You're not a fix-it pixie. Not the Fixer. It's not what you do . . . right?"

He put down the shortbread. "It's not what I do — but I'll do it for you. I'd do anything in the world for you."

"Dinnae be a numpty," she said, shaking her head at him. "Ye barely know me, laddie, and I've caused ye nothing but grief."

"You used your wish for me — and you saw *me*. Not him."

"Yes, about that." She wanted to ask about the wish embroidered on the scrap of tartan cloth, but another desire was more urgent. "Why don't I remember Mitch's face? It bothers me."

"I don't know, but I believe he blames me, because you saw *me* first. Perhaps your soul saw me as a whole person, and so he became the shadow — the non-person — to you."

"That's just creepy. And it's not so. I *do* see you as a whole — real — person, James. I've remembered you for a year and I knew you right away tonight. But I've spent far more time with Mitch."

She felt a blush rising into her cheeks as she recalled how she'd spent some of that time.

His grey eyes narrowed. "What are you thinking about, my queen?"

"Just remembering."

"I can guess what," he said, dryly. "I remember too. He tried to keep me out, but I *do* remember." He got up. "If I help you with the bats . . . if they are bats . . . will you give me a kiss? One that's all for me? You can close your eyes with me, because you know my face."

Queenie shook her head. "I don't trade for kisses, James. And as I said, you hardly know me."

"To hardly know you is to love you," he misquoted.

"Dinnae be so gowkish."

He favoured her with a brief and wistful smile. "At least you didn't bash my heid with a besom for asking."

"I think you'd better go."

"After we see to the bats, my love."

"I told you—"

"And *I* told *you*. I'll do anything for you, even if you won't kiss me. Even if you never want to see me again, please let me do this one thing for you."

Chapter Eleven: Wards

Queenie Hart, Mid-October, 2021

Queenie fought a brief battle with herself. She needed to be independent, but James was here, and he was willing.

She hated to take advantage of his feelings for her, but it made sense to accept help for things she couldn't do herself.

She capitulated. "Aye, then, and thank ye kindly. Come and see wha' the trouble is."

She tucked her *aide-mémoire* into the pocket of her jacket. She'd put it back in the frame, and when Mitch returned, she'd have that talk he'd wanted. And she'd apologise in her most heartfelt manner for being such a sheepheided bitch to him.

James followed her obediently to the narthex.

"Listen," Queenie said, indicating the door.

She remembered her expectation that the sounds would be gone if she got Mitch along to fix it, but the scratching and fluttering was still going on.

It wasn't as creepy, now that she had company.

"Do ye hear that?"

"Yes—probably better than you," he said. He grasped the rope handle with one hand as she had done, and he tugged.

Queenie was sure he was stronger than she was, but the door stayed shut.

He put his shoulder against it, and he pushed.

The door creaked, but it stayed shut.

"Well!" James stood back and folded his arms. The action

made the sweater tighten across his broad shoulders. He was taller and broader than Mitch.

She wondered if he was doing it on purpose.

Mitch doesn't posture.

A sense of the lanky figure she knew . . . okay, that she *loved* . . . flitted across her mind. The face was averted.

She jerked her attention back to the handsome laddie before her.

"Can you conjure it open?" She remembered what he'd said before. "I give you full permission." And then, seeing the light flare into his eyes, and an odd shift in his expression begin, she added quickly, "to open this door, I mean."

He turned aside, as if to re-examine the door. "I can certainly try, but I suspect it's been closed and warded by someone exceedingly strong."

"I thought about using an axe, or a hacksaw, but then I remembered I'm not supposed to make structural changes to The Belfry."

He grinned at her. "Queenie, that's what I love so much about you."

She backed off.

He continued, "That mix of kindness and invective, and the violent impulses tempered by common sense. You're a glorious mixture—a beautiful enigma. You're *my* beautiful enigma."

"Can you try conjuring?" she persisted.

"Yes." He put his hands on the door and he closed his eyes.

Queenie saw his long eyelashes catch copper glints from the ceiling light.

His eyes popped open, and he stood back and held out his hands. "I'm sorry, love. It won't work."

"Can you try again?"

"I could try until the kine come hame, but it won't work. There are two reasons why. One is ethical. This is not my door, and although you gave me permission, you're not technically the owner — in fact, you're proscribed from forcing this door by the very fact that it's been closed off. The other problem is more mechanical. Someone warded this, and he — or she — doesn't expect or want it to be unwarded. That someone is *exceedingly* strong and determined."

Queenie recalled Mitch saying something about wards or warding, and she resolved to look it up in *The Fay Companion*. She'd read quite a bit of it, but terms were only memorable if she had a reason to know them.

"I suppose if I can't get in, they can't get out," she said. She added, "That bothers me. I dinnae want bats in ma hair, or roostin' in ma closet, or leaving shite in ma kitchen, but neither do I want the wee beasties to suffer."

"If they are bats, they probably have a way out through the tower."

"But why are these beasties suddenly scratching about *now*? I've lived here for a couple o' months, with nae but an occasional flutter or scritch . . .an' that I put doon to the birds on the tower."

He put his ear to the door again.

"I don't know. Maybe *he* would know, but I don't. I'm sorry I can't be him for you, love."

He sounded genuinely regretful.

"Never mind," Queenie said. "I have a good idea who might be able to help us — if he will."

"Oh?"

"Oh, yes. It was probably he who did whatever was done in the first place. It has his finger marks all over it." She struck the door with her palm. "Yah clarty bawbaggus! Shut yer geggie!"

The rustling stopped.

James looked at her with respect. "Great bogle, even *I* cannae unravel that, dearie!"

Queenie shrugged. Neither could she.

She felt unexpectedly calm because now she had a plan.

"James, I have to call someone in the morning, after nine. I'd quite like you to be here, because I might need help explaining, or understanding the response."

He smiled delightedly. "I'll be here! Whistle and I'll come to you! And that's *me* talking, and not *him*."

It trembled on her lips to invite him to stay for the rest of the night. She'd done it with Mitch, and he *was* Mitch—sort of. Yet Mitch would be back in a while and then she'd not see James again for almost a year—if she ever did. And Mitch would know, and he'd remember, and it would be just too weird for words.

She said, "If you come before nine, we can have breakfast together and plan our campaign."

He nodded, gave her a longing look, and turned to the outer door.

Queenie didn't really want him to leave. She'd had no one to talk to for a while, but it was unfair to keep him here just for that. She stood back and watched him down the steps.

"Lock up behind me, dear love," he called, and a minute later she heard Ethel's motor start.

Dear love. That's a new one.

She wondered again if James had a driver's licence. However could he have picked up the requisite number of hours' experience to sit the test?

It would be *too* bizarre if James were one of the fay folk Branok helped with starter papers. She wished she could ask, but she knew Branok wouldn't tell her. Maybe James would, if she phrased it properly. Maybe he'd explain that embroidered tartan wish. She still had it, tucked away in the bottom of Great-Grandmother Mary's Cloisonne vase along with pens and paperclips, Great-Grandmother Victoria's bracelet, a coin from the year of her birth, and other odds and ends.

How utterly bizarre to be a person for one month of the year.

She shivered.

And I thought I *had it hard.*

Back in bed, she lay trying not to hear the sounds in the belltower. She wasn't afraid of bats, but what if it were something else?

Mitch would have been able to fix it.

Eventually, she slept, only to wake to weak spring sunshine streaming through the stained-glass window, turning the bed to blue and red and gold and to the sense of someone watching her.

She stretched and then she turned her head and gave a squeal of mingled fright and outrage. "James Stuart! What the *feck* are you doing here, you muttonheid?"

He smiled across at her from his perch on a chair he must have brought up from the main room.

"I was watching you sleep, my love."

She sat up, clutching the quilt to her chest. "Ye'd better not hae been here all nicht!"

"Only for an hour or so. You *said* I could come for breakfast."

"I know fu' weel what I said!" She bit her cheek to hold back a giggle. "Get yer impertinent bollocks doonstairs into the kitchen!"

"I'm going." He got out of the chair, neat and combed as if he were fresh from a long night of sleep and half an hour in the bathroom. She wondered if he ever wore anything else but the argyle sweater and cords.

"Take the chair with ye!" she added.

He kissed his fingers and the chair vanished.

Queenie uttered another squeal of shock. She seized her pillow and threw it at him. "Get oot!"

He fled.

Queenie decided to leave her shower until he'd gone. She looked distastefully at the crumpled tee and old leggings she'd had on last night and she dressed instead in a chaste grey pinafore over a blue plaid blouse. She brushed her hair and tied it back, resisting the desire to look in the mirror. She knew she didn't look anything like as neat as James.

No one looked as neat as James.

She went down to the kitchen to find her guest making oatmeal and tea. A bowl of blueberries sat on the counter, along with a jar of something that was possibly yoghourt but more likely cream.

"I asked *you* to breakfast, laddie," she said.

He turned to beam at her. "I wanted to do something nice for you."

"Because it's what you do?"

"It's not. It's what *he* does. But I wanted to, for you."

He'd commandeered Great-Granny Mary Hart's vase for a fat bunch of violets and freesias, and their perfume spread through the kitchen like the essence of spring.

"Mmm, heavenly," Queenie said, breathing them in. "But what did you do with the stuff that was already in it?"

"It's all safe, in a drawer." He indicated the dresser. He gave her a sideways look. "You kept my wish."

"I thought it was *my* wish."

"It was, but you used it for me."

"About that . . . about the tartan cloth . . . the embroidery," she began, but at that moment James brought the bowls of porridge to the table and offered her the blueberries, still covered with the bloom and sweetness of the sun.

They've never been in a fridge.

In the exchange of berries and cream . . . it *was* cream . . . she couldn't find a chink to ask about the wish.

It was decidedly pleasant to have breakfast with someone. The lassie haggis came and went in her voice, but James didn't seem bothered. He talked eagerly about his parents and his cousin, Georgiana, and the dog he'd loved for years.

"Horace was *my* dog. Georgiana took care of him when I was away, but he always remembered me."

Queenie identified his cousin as the person who had

loaned her a tricycle.

She said, cautiously, "So Georgiana knows about you?"

His eyes widened. "Yes, obviously. Why wouldn't she?"

"I thought—"

"You thought I was a secret, aye?"

"Weel—aye."

"Not from Georgie. We've known one another since I came to *be*. She gave me Horace for my own. Her man and her bairns know me . . . *Auncle Jamie,* the wee ones call me."

Auncle. That was another of the odd terms Queenie had learned from her perusal of *The Fay Companion.* It was an inclusive form to mean aunt or uncle.

She couldn't think what on earth to say to that. She wondered if he had ever had a girlfriend. He couldn't have a wife, or a family, and only a part-time dog. She wondered what had happened to Horace, since James spoke of him in the past tense. She knew the fourteen or so years of a dog's life was never enough for the bereft owners left behind, but what had James and Horace had? A few widely spaced months?

"What's wrong?" he asked.

She shook her head, unable to ask or to keep back her pity if she thought too much about it. "It's after nine. It's time to make that call. I'll put it on speaker because I want you to listen in, in case I need some help with interpreting the fairy stuff."

He waited expectantly.

Queenie keyed in the familiar number, and she put the phone on video call.

"Queenie! Everything okay?" Andy asked, leaning into the pick-up.

"Aye, but I'm wishfu' to speak with Oliver. Is he there?"

"He's—"

"Less of the *he*," Oliver's voice cut in. The phone rocked and shifted and then the face of a distinguished old man appeared. He was handsome in an austere way, but there was something slightly raffish about the set of his mouth. He wore a short silver earring in one ear, as had all the piskies Queenie had knowingly encountered. He didn't look ninety-six.

"Greet you, Miss Hart, I see you are even more comely than Androw described. What may I do for you?"

Queenie said, "Good morning, Oliver." She supposed she should have said *Master Porthwellian,* but it was too late now. He was irrevocably *Oliver* to her. "I have a — a laddie here with me." She tilted the phone and beckoned James into the pick-up. "This is James Stuart. James, this gentleman is Oliver Porthwellian. He used to live in The Belfry, and he's more or less my landlord. One of them."

Oliver nodded. "More rather than less. I hope you are still comfortable in my old home, Miss Hart."

"Yes, I love it. I'll stay forever if you'll let me."

If a man of ninety-six found *forever* a confronting thought, Oliver showed no signs of it in his face. Indeed, he looked gratified.

"Listen, Oliver —"

"I am listening, Miss Hart."

"I've been trying to get into the belltower, but the door is jammed shut."

"It is not." Oliver focused behind Queenie, evidently looking at James. "I'm sure Master Stuart has told you that already. Braesider, am I right, laddie?"

"Aye," James said. "At least, I identify as such."

"Piffle. Either you are a braeman or you aren't, and you *are.* You're as brae as they come, despite the glamour to your eyes. And therefore, you know at least as much as is good for you about doors that don't open."

James leaned forward, warm against Queenie's shoulder, tucking an arm around her so naturally she barely registered his action. "Master Porthwellian, I did tell Queenie I thought the door was warded."

"Thought, nothing. Piffle, I say! You *knew*."

"Aye, I knew."

Queenie said, "Why?"

"To keep meddling humans away from Kerensa's bells," Oliver said readily.

Queenie heard a dismayed squeak, presumably from Dellion. "Grandad! You *can't* say that to Queenie!"

"Can I not? I was of the impression I just had," Oliver said.

Dellion's face bobbed into view. "Queenie, I'm *sorry*. I know I'm not always appropriate, but *he's* not fit to be let out. Humans are no more meddlers than we are — sometimes not so much."

Queenie said, "I'm no' all human, Dellion, as you know fu' weel."

Oliver pressed his great-granddaughter out of the way. "Do I detect a goodly dollop of braeside lassie, my dear? Very, very nice. No wonder your tarts . . . and your upper assets . . . are so fine."

"Never mind ma bluid, or ma titties," Queenie said. "I ken fine ye're a wicked auld mannie, Oliver Porthwellian. Mesh yer feckie or I'll ha' at ye with ma besom acrost yer ba-hoochie!"

Oliver shied back. "Great bogle!"

James said, "She can't help it, master."

"I am mortally sure she *can* if she so chooses," Oliver disagreed. He frowned and then his eyes lit with evil intent. "But I'd not have her so choose. There's something delightful about a maid with a large and piquant vocabulary, as well as a large — "

"Granddad! No!" Dellion all but screamed.

Queenie took a deep breath. "I don't intend to meddle with the belltower, but there are beasties in there scritchin' and scratchin' fit to wake the deid. I want them oot!"

Oliver's patrician face creased into a wholly wicked smile. "Then want must be your master, my fine buxom lassie."

Another squeak from Dellion assured Queenie Oliver was as far over the line as she thought he was.

She pointed her finger at him. "Any more o' that, ye evil auld mannie, an' ye can *whistle* for tarts to sweeten yer final days."

Oliver's grin grew even wider. "Oh, a maid after my own heart, Miss Hart. If I were sixty years younger — and a single man — I'd lay you well."

"Granddad!" wailed Dellion again.

James said quickly, "Master Porthwellian, are those beasties in the belfry fay bats?"

Oliver nodded. "Yes, I brought 'em over through the cove gate when we moved in. Place was called The Belfry, so bats there had to be. Only for All Hallows, though. It amused my minx, my Kerensa, to have them roosting up there among her bells." He fixed his gaze on Queenie. "Come November, they'll flit back through the cave and go *over there* to play tickle and flitch with the bogles. *No harm.*"

"Oh, really?"

"I can't suppose a fine lassie such as yourself would be worried by a few bats."

"Noo, but I'm worried about the bat shite."

"Then after All Hallows you have my permission to go into the belltower and clean it up — get your swain to do it if you're too delicate. Just treat Kerensa's bells with proper respect."

"The door is stuck fast," Queenie reminded him.

"I'll visit you and unstick it, come November," Oliver said. "That's if I'm still around. If I go to glory before then, you have my permission to take it down with an axe. I'll be beyond caring then."

CHAPTER TWELVE: TARTAN TARTS

Queenie Hart, Mid-October, 2021

After that, Andy got hold of the phone and looked apologetically at Queenie.

"I hope this little exchange hasn't caused you too much unease. Oliver can behave respectably if he cares to. There must be something about the sight of you that loosens his inhibitions," he said. He rolled his eyes. *"What* a performance!"

"It's nae my responsibility, and ye're no' ye're partner's keeper, and I gave him a wee serve back. Andy, did you know about the bats?"

"I did not. Oliver never saw fit to tell me. It may explain why previous tenants haven't stayed beyond the three months' minimum. Er — will you?"

"Try to get me oot an' see where it gets ye," she said.

"A besom to the bahoochie?" Andy gave his delightful smile.

"No' for you. Never for you. I ken fine ye're a friend."

"Good. Dellion and I see you as a friend, too. We always shall. Therefore, I'll undertake to get Oliver to you on November the first to unward the door, and I'll send him up the stair *first* to spring any surprises and to flush out any lingering winged beasties. Until then, please restrain yourself from having at the door with an axe."

"All right then. I'll ignore the wee beasties if ye're sure they're in nae distress."

"What would you do if I said I wasn't sure?"

"I'd hae Duncan Dee bring me an axe wi' the next order from Fiddle-de-Dee and be damned to your *please restrain.*"

"Then I *am* sure," Andy said. "If that's all—"

"Aye, for noo."

"*Nos da*," he said, and the call ended.

Queenie said to James, "What does he mean by that?"

"He doesn't want you to chop holes in the door."

"No, *nos da*."

"It's a pisky farewell." He gave her a squeeze with the arm that was still around her. "That old pisky man is a thorough-going twenty-four carat, point nine-nine-nine silver, brass-knobbed, copper-bottomed terror."

Queenie said, "I like him, the auld deil. I thought he was so gentlemanly . . . and then he breaks oot and speaks o' *laying me. If he were a single man* indeed. Is he not?"

"I would think his minx has gone to glory, but he still feels wed to her," James said.

"His minx would be his wee wifie?"

"Yes. Kerensa, if I heard it right. A fine old pisky name."

"Then wha's wi' all the inappropriate talk?"

"He's a pisky man," James said, as if that explained it.

"About that. I'm not trying to be offensive, but how are you a braeside laddie if Mitch is a pixie man? Isn't it a matter of genetics?"

"Aye, but you see Danna—our mother—is a lassie. Danna Stuart from Braeside . . . and her mother Elspeth was a Campbell lassie. Beaman—our dad—is a pixie man from the pixie forest. Instead of wedding a pixie miss in the approved fashion, he found himself what he terms *a grand armful of a lassie.* We two threw different ways."

"I see. Georgiana is your cousin, but do you have any brothers or sisters?"

To her surprise, he said he did. "Three sisters, Afton, Blossom, and Hazel . . . all pixie misses, all much older and wed with families. I call them the sistren."

She remembered he had mentioned that word before. She *must* learn to listen more closely.

He added, "*He* was a surprise packet when Mum was already forty."

"And I expect *you* were even more of one."

"Yes." He tilted his head to rest his cheek against her hair. "Mum—"

"I expect your mum was pleased, since you're like her," Queenie said. She hitched her shoulder, smelling the warm, clean scent of wool. "James, what are you doing?"

"Encroaching," he said, stepping away.

"Thank you for helping me out with Oliver," Queenie said.

"I was glad to. I expect you want me to go away now."

"Not unless you want to. I'm going to make some tartan tarts and I need a tester."

She hadn't been going to, but now it seemed a good idea.

"I'll stay a while," James said readily. He looked up at the clock. "I have to meet the train at midday."

"I see. Where do you live?"

"At the *pied-a-terre*. I can't have my own house. It wouldn't be practical."

He sounded matter of fact, but Queenie felt another surge of compassion for him. She supposed Mitch, as the main self, had to have the say in where they lived, but poor James had so little of his own. No wonder he had that bee in his bonnet about *I saw you first.*

"Do you always wear those clothes?" she asked.

If the change of subject startled him, he didn't show it. "Why not? I don't need many—they don't have time to wear out. *He* wouldn't wear them. They wouldn't fit."

"You never wear a kilt?"

He paused and then he said gently, "Mum made me this sweater. It's a pattern from Granny Elspeth's family. I have

89

three in the same style."

"That's not an answer. *Do* you ever wear a kilt? The truth noo, or I'll have at ye with ma besom!"

"Have you even got a besom, my dearest?"

Queenie frowned. That thought had never occurred to her before. "I *feel* as if I hae one. A braw fine one wi' heather twigs, fit for boxin' the ears o' impertinent laddies."

"Well, the truth is, I do have a kilt. Blue-grey Stuart tartan. Auld Donald Stuart — Mum's da — gave it to me as a gift when *he* got enough years . . . turned eighteen, I mean."

"Oh! I'd love to see it. Would you wear it for me?"

She thought he'd be pleased, but he narrowed his eyes. "You said you wouldn't trade for kisses."

"I willnae!" she flashed.

"I suppose I'd wear it if I had the occasion, but it's not what one wears to drive a bus in Fiddle Bay. I don't want to look ridiculous."

Queenie thought the same could be said about argyle sweaters. She couldn't remember seeing any other man under seventy wearing one of those.

"If there were to be an occasion . . . if I happened to find one where a kilt would be *appropriate* . . . would you?"

"Then yes, I'd wear it for you."

"Not for yoursel'?"

"For myself also. It's been such a long while . . ."

His voice faded, and she understood how difficult it must be from his perspective to work out elapsed time.

They left the subject alone by silent consent, and Queenie began work on the tartan tarts. "These would be fun for Burns Night, maybe," she said.

"I won't be here then."

"No."

"*He* will."

"I doubt Mitch would have an interest in Burns Night."

"Neither have I any interest, except in the academic sense, since I have never been around for one," he said dryly. "No doubt he'll eat the tarts, however."

She thought of something else she wanted to know. "Oliver said something about your eyes, and a glamour."

"Oliver said a great deal that was maybe better unsaid."

She pursued the subject. "I read about glamours in my books. They're sort of like conjuring, but they make others think they see something they don't . . . or stop them from seeing something, maybe."

"That's a fair enough summation."

His voice was even, so apparently he, unlike Mitch, had no problem with her researching the fay.

"What did he mean about your eyes?"

James looked at her and then away. It reminded her suddenly of Mitch, as he hadn't done before, and a pang shot through her.

I'm letting James keep me company while I make tarts. I wouldnae allow Mitch that . . . I stormed at him instead.

James said, "I can show you, if you want."

"I want."

"It will look — odd to you. Maybe frightening."

"I won't be frightened."

"All right. I suppose you wouldn't kiss me first?"

"We've been through that."

"No, dearie, but you see — this effect is generally tied to high emotion. I could raise some remarkably high emotion if you were to kiss me."

"In that case, never mind. Maybe you should just go."

His eyes widened, flared, and the loch-grey colour shimmered and changed to a shifting patina of silver, lavender, purple . . .

Queenie stared in awe.

He'd been beautiful before, but with his eyes doing — whatever they were doing — he was breathtaking.

She became aware that her mouth had dropped open.

James blinked, kissed his fingers, and the shimmer faded, leaving his eyes the clear grey of before. "You didn't squeal," he said.

"Noo — that was so bonnie — magical — what was it?"

"It's called *heathering*," he said. "Didn't you see it in your book?"

She shook her head.

"Then maybe it's in its own entry rather than with the main braefolk one."

She said, "Obviously, you didnae need a kiss after all."

"Strong emotion brings it out. You asked me to go — "

"It wasnae a threat," she said uncomfortably.

"No, my love. I realised that, but my heart misgave me." He looked at the clock. "It really is time to go. I have a bus to drive."

A lump came into Queenie's throat, but she smiled and said she would see him later.

He took himself off, and she continued with her baking. After a while, she telephoned Fiddle-de-Dee and asked Duncan if he would bring her some smoked haddock, a sack of oatmeal, loose leaf tea, a crate of neeps, a sheep's heid and —

"*Neeps?*"

"Aye, turnips."

"I have those, but a sheep's head?" he said doubtfully.

"Nae?"

"Not much call for such things in Fiddle Bay. We tried stocking tripe and dripping and brawn in the deli, but no one would touch them — the black pudding went green. We had to burn sage and exorcise it."

"I'll make do wi' pigs' trotters then. Ye *do* have those?"

"Not until Monday and then I'd have to get my supplier to remove them from the pig," he said.

Queenie forced herself to focus. She perceived Duncan was

trying to be funny, so she laughed.

"Never mind. It was just a wild idea. Duncan, does the offer of stocking tarts still stand?"

"Very much so," he said, apparently happy to be on less esoteric grounds. "I'll bring your order myself after seven, if that suits, and pick up the tarts. Are you really okay, Queenie?"

"Aye, I am. It's gey kind o' ye to ask it."

"If you leave the tarts in the hatch, I can pick them up without disturbing you, but remember, if you ever need someone to just talk with, my wife will come," he said, and he ended the call.

Queenie blew out her cheeks. Duncan's wife Willow was a softly spoken person with a sweet smile, and maybe when the witching month was over, she would invite her for tea and tarts to set Duncan's sympathetic heart at rest.

She couldn't do it yet, however.

She felt restless. She wished she had that besom, so she could give The Belfry a right guid sweep out and bang the door to quieten the beasties in the belltower. She had a vacuum cleaner, but that wasn't the same thing.

A besom was what she longed for.

Duncan delivered her groceries quietly, with just a discreet knock at her door. "Okay in there, Queenie?"

"Aye, I'm bonnie," she sang out.

When she was sure he'd gone, she opened the door and carried in the boxes and sacks. He'd brought everything but the trotters, although he'd added chicken drumsticks to the order as a substitute.

It was a kind thought, she supposed.

On top of the order she found the new edition of the *Stradevarious*.

She sat in the kitchen with a cup of tea brewed from the loose leaves, listening to the rustling of the bats in the belltower, and reading the *Strad.* She hoped and half expected

James would let himself in as he had that morning, but nine o'clock came and went.

And I won't call him. It wouldnae be fair.

She wished she could speak with his mother, or the accommodating Cousin Georgiana, but she didn't have their numbers. She had no idea of Georgiana's surname, or of those of the three sisters — Blossom, Afton and . . . was it Hazel? And although she looked for Beaman and Danna Kingsolver she found no digital footprint. James had said they didn't use phones much.

Anyway, wha' could I say? I lay with your pixie son, and I know the October laddie?

She was tempted to ask Gillan for advice, since she, too, lived as two beings, but Gillan's case was different. It was apparent she could transform into and out of Lady Velvet whenever she chose, whereas Mitch and James had no choice. What was it like for them? Mitch knew the change was coming, and he had made provision for it, but what was it like, going to sleep one night and waking as another person with different imperatives, different tastes, and another face and form? If the change happened at midnight, did they stand in front of a mirror and watch the transformation come in with dread and denial? Did they strip naked first, so as not to manifest in clothing too big or too small?

It must be worse for James, who had so little time to be independent.

To distract herself, she turned up the contents page of the *Strad* and found a whole section devoted to Halloween. She remembered Maureen Tucker speaking of local celebrations, so she turned to the section to see what was going on in her new hometown.

Pumpkin carving at the village green.

Cats and Kits Yoga.

Mums' Run with a fancy-dress race.

Dad Ballet performing excerpts from Drozdov's All Hallows

Eve *in the town hall.*

Broomstick jousting on the green.

Lucky Cauldron in Fiddle-de-Dee for the kids.

Queenie's eyebrows rose higher with every item of the program. The people of Fiddle Bay were certifiable.

But then, who was she to point a besom at anyone for being odd?

The last item was comparatively normal.

Fancy-dress Halloween Ball at Oakengrove . . . eight o'clock on the 31st of October. Ends at midnight. Pumpkin soup will be served. Bring a plate for dessert.

Queenie read that one over again.

Could she — aye, she could.

Any odd behaviour would be in character.

But she needed a costume.

Of course, she would go all-out *lassie haggis.*

The thought filled her with a fierce joy.

She called Nona Tilbury, who was understandably surprised to hear from her so late in the evening.

Once they'd established it wasn't an emergency, Nona heard her out. Although sympathetic to her cause, she said to the best of her knowledge there were no costume hire places in Fiddle Bay. "If you wanted to buy one—"

"No' synthetic tat," Queenie said. She knew she needed good Scottish wool and leather. Aye, and a besom.

"No, love. This is a little place in the city . . . down at The Rocks. Do you know where I mean?"

"Aye," she said cautiously.

"The shop's in Lady Lane. It's called Fairings, and it can be a bit difficult to find. I know people who've walked straight past it three or four times. Sounds mad, I know."

It sounded perfectly reasonable to Queenie.

"If you can find it, they'll have exactly what you want. They always do." She paused and then she said, "I got my absolutely favourite dress there. I was pregnant with our second, and I was feeling frowsty and frumpy and a bit light-headed. I went into the shop mainly to get out of the sun and put my head together, but I came out with *the* most gorgeous spiral-pleated dress in the prettiest shades of lilac and blue. These days I wear it with a belt when I feel the need of a bit of cheering up. My husband loves it, and that's a first, because mostly men and women have very different tastes when it comes to clothes. If you go to the shop, if you can find it, ask for what you want."

Queenie's heart gave her a qualm when she thought of returning to the city while in the grip of the Caledonian Curse, but then — what had she to fear? It was the folk of Fiddle Bay she dealt with these days and mustn't offend. Sydney could go fash itself.

She'd gone to the quay once before when the alternative was worse. She could do the same again.

"I'll go, then," she said.

"You do that. Is that all?" Nona sounded dry, and so Queenie thanked her and rang off.

Halloween was closing in, and she had no time to waste.

"Nae time like the present," she told herself. It was much too late to head down to the city now, but she promised herself she'd go in the morning.

Chapter Thirteen: Thunder

Queenie Hart, October, 2021

Queenie almost expected James to be sitting on the chair watching her when she woke to the rustlings from the belltower, but she was alone in the room.

The light coming through the high windows seemed dull, but she was determined to follow through on her impulse of the night before.

She ate a hasty breakfast and then she returned to her room to dress for her trip to the city.

She had taken one step down the shallow stair when a crash overhead made her jump.

The roof's falling in.

She tilted her face up, dreading to see a crack spreading across the ceiling. It could happen. The old rectory that had stood between the graveyard and The Belfry had been pulled down after a tree fell through its roof.

The dark trees.

Crash! A harsh flicker of light dazzled her as it shot through the stained glass.

Only a thunderstorm.

I can wait it out.

Crash!

Not even night-time.

Crash!

Flash!

Peering up, she mis-stepped, and the next moment, her

foot came down awkwardly on the leading edge of the riser. She rocked, staggered, tried to recover herself — and fell.

It might have been much worse. The stair was shallow, so she didn't have far to fall, but the wind was knocked out of her, and she came down heavily, wrenching both ankles as she landed.

"Och! What a haunless glaikit eejit ye are!" she exclaimed when the scene steadied.

She tried to scramble to her feet, but her ankles howled their protest.

"Black Snitch fly away wi' ye!" she yelled in frustration, and she added, "Ow!"

Crash! The thunder added its comment to her situation.

Queenie stayed where she was for a while. She knew from experience that *hurt* was not necessarily *harm*. That was one of Liberty Hart's self-help maxims, somewhere along the lines of *sticks and stones.*

Didn't hit ma heid. Nothing's broken.

She was sure of that. The pain was sharp and insistent, but she hadn't felt anything snap.

After the first shock receded, she tried to get up.

No luck.

There were no banisters, for the broad, shallow steps leading to the mezzanine level didn't require them. Therefore, there was no solid structure she could use to haul herself to her feet.

She waited a while longer.

Call the Fixer.

I'm in a fix.

Another one? He'd say that with amusement in his voice, but his tone would turn to concern when he understood she was hurt and not just wanting his attention.

He's not here.

Call James, then.

He's not the Fixer. He'd think —

She wouldn't let herself know what he'd think.

If I called him, would it be to get me out of this fix, or whistle and I'll come to ye?

She hated second-guessing her motives, her intentions, and her desires. She hated stirring *his* desires.

Until *this* October she'd thought she was a good person, if she thought about herself at all. She knew she didn't behave well while under the Caledonian Curse, but aside from that, she tried to be kind and fair and generous as far as it lay in her power to be.

Her dealings with Mitch had shown her otherwise.

I was unjust and unkind to him. I was cauld and hard when he begged to come to me and talk things over.

Aye, but he pushed ye back for his cat's convenience.

And that gave ye *the right to tell him it was no' convenient to hae him by while ye made tarts?*

She'd let James stay while she made the tartan tarts . . .in fact, she'd invited him.

Call him now.

Ow.

She wondered if this painful fall was in some way her punishment for the way she'd acted to both men.

Costumes indeed.

Having no one to depend on but herself, she got to her hands and knees and shuffled down the rest of the steps. With her palms braced on the third step from the bottom and her feet on the floor, she managed to get upright, but the idea of walking felt implausible. Neither ankle would take her full weight, so she couldn't take a step.

She manoeuvred so she was sitting on the bottom riser, and she leaned forwards to examine the damage.

The outer joint on her right ankle was grazed, with a few dots of blood already setting like hard, shiny red rhinestones. The other foot *looked* all right, but she felt an ominous heat and puffiness.

Her shoe was uncomfortably tight, so she eased it off.

The thunder went on crashing, and the lightning flickered wickedly. She imagined hearing it sizzle.

What if it struck the belltower?

What if The Belfry caught fire and she was helpless?

I could use ma besom as a crutch . . .

Nonsense, Queenie Hart. In fact, piffle *as Oliver would say. You don't have a besom. You have —*

She had her dear Fixer. He'd come to her. Except he was *unavailable* for the next eleven days and angry with her anyway.

A strange sensation against her hip made her jump uneasily before she identified it as her phone, competing with the crash of thunder.

She fished it out. "Aye?"

A familiar voice spoke in her ear, but she couldn't make out what it said.

"I cannae hear ye over the thunner an' lichnin," she explained.

Crash!

Spiiiit!

She waited for the next clash but instead there was a sudden eerie silence.

Eye of the storm.

She waited, but there was nothing.

Hae I gone deif?

Then came that familiar voice. "Can you hear me now, Queenie love?"

"James." A mix of relief and annoyance flooded her.

She'd deliberately not called him, and now here was he calling her.

He said, "I'm just outside. I have a delivery for you. It's coming down in auld wives and pike staves out here, so I don't want to leave it out in the weather."

Queenie was about to tell him to stop havering and bring

it in, when she recalled that she hadn't made an order. Not consciously, anyway.

"What delivery?" she asked.

"Just a wee one."

"It's not sheep's heid and pluck, is it?"

"No, dearie."

"Bring it in then," she said.

She ended the call and pocketed her phone.

From the foot of the mezzanine steps she could see her kitchen but not the main room, which was beyond a dividing wall. She leaned forwards and wrapped her arms around her knees, in a parody of the way she'd been sitting when James came to her summons about bats in the belfry.

"Queenie?" She heard his call from the main room. Something caught the corner of her eye in the kitchen, and she understood she was seeing the delivery arrive.

He must have come in and then conjured it . . .

He could just as well hae done that from ootside.

"Thank you," she called.

The order looked odd, even from where she was. Instead of the boxes and sacks Duncan Dee used for packing, this one was in a large basket.

A puppy? Did I order a Scottie? A Westie? A collie or a deer-hound?

Her heart gave a skip.

Angel Petty, her former landlady at Mother Goose Lane in Sydney, had denied her request to be allowed to keep a dog, but she could have one at The Belfry!

Even as her hope rose, she realised it was most unlikely that a pup would arrive in a basket of this kind. It was a wide-mouthed willow basket with a hooped handle and a loosely fitting lid.

Besides, hadn't Gillan St Ives said no one could conjure sentient creatures?

The door in the divider opened, and James stepped in, trim

and neat and dry.

His gaze fell on her, and his grey eyes lit up. He came towards her with his hands outstretched as if to help her up.

"Wait." Queenie held up one hand, palm outwards.

"I'm sorry. I wasn't going to grab you." He stopped and then he added, wistfully, "I'm just so happy to see you."

"I'm gey glad to see you, too, laddie," Queenie said, relief outweighing her ambivalence. She indicated her shoeless foot. "I took a wee tumble doon the stairs when the thunner feart me."

He came closer. "Are you much hurt, love?"

"No' so bad. Nothing broken. I just cannae—" Her voice broke.

"Can't get up," he said. He turned and sat on the step beside her, and she felt his gaze on her.

She looked up, aware of the warmth of his shoulder and the scent of freshly washed and dried wool.

He kept looking at her, his grey eyes shimmering gently with the heather colours.

"What?" she asked.

He chuckled unexpectedly. "Well, love, you didn't want me to help you up, so I thought I'd just sit here with you and bathe in the delight of the thought you won't run away from me this time because you can't."

"That's no' so chivalrous o' ye. Mitch would have me up on the couch wi' my feet in his lap," she said reproachfully. "Aye, an' he'd conjure liniment to soothe my hurt."

"Is that what you want?"

"I dinnae want to sit here forever," she said. She resisted the urge to lean against him.

"I'll help you up." He got to his feet. "What will it be, my dearie? I can sweep you into my arms or support you while you hobble."

Queenie weighed up the choices. Both would be

embarrassing. She preferred to move under her own steam, but if she cried out or, worse, cursed in lassie haggis, that would be undignified.

Besides . . .

"If you could carry me to the kitchen, that would be fine. Aye, an' get me some ice," she said.

James bent and scooped Queenie into his arms with no apparent effort.

Her brows shot up. She'd known he must be strong, but she'd never been lifted this way since childhood.

Her heart fluttered.

He adjusted his grip and gave her a cheeky grin. "Now, I can carry you off and have my wicked way with you."

"Aye, and I could tip a pan o' Scotch broth over yer heid," Queenie responded.

"You haven't got any."

"Hae I no'?" At that moment she was unsure of what she had . . . or hadn't got in the kitchen. Her head was spinning, her feet were hurting, and everything in between just wanted to stay in this man's arms.

"Well, have you?"

Queenie sighed, gave into temptation and leaned her head against his shoulder. "Noo," she said sadly.

"Then let's make some while we wait for the storm to ease."

She thought it *had* eased, but she concentrated on not whimpering as her ankles shrieked about being unsupported in the air.

James carried her to the kitchen, and she was very much startled when one of the chairs from the main room appeared. He set her down in it without comment and then he conjured one of the kitchen chairs over and lifted her feet onto it.

When Mitch conjured, aside from the time he'd stripped naked at her request, he did it discreetly. *Blink and ye'll miss it.*

James was more flamboyant and much less concerned about tossing things about in public . . . in her presence, anyway.

He stood looking at Queenie, arranged like a fainting Victorian maiden across two chairs. "Do you want me to get that other shoe off?"

"Maybe."

He unlaced the brogue and very gently eased it off her foot.

"Do you want that ice, or will you try some of Mum's marigold sovereign?"

"You haven't got any."

"Hae I no'?"

"Well, have you?" she asked.

"Let's see." James made his kissing gesture and was suddenly holding an opaque ceramic pot. He showed it to her. "*He* keeps it at the *pied-a-terre* for application to damaged damsels," he said.

"I'm no damsel." Queenie wriggled her toes and flinched. The initial grinding pain had eased, but there was an ominous stiffness that suggested her feet and ankles were planning something monumental in the bruised-and-swollen department.

"No, my dear love. You're no damsel. You're my bonnie lassie, even though I'm not allowed to claim you."

James lifted her feet and slid underneath them into the chair, so her heels were in his lap. "This might hurt a bit, but I promise you it will help," he said, reverting to the practicalities.

A crack of thunder made Queenie jolt uneasily.

"The storm's back," she said.

"It never went away." James took the lid off the pot and Queenie smelled a sweet, tangy scent, redolent of hot summer evenings in an herb garden.

"Mum had this recipe from an old lassie named Emer

Inkersoll," he said, as lightning flickered. "She was a lovely woman — went to glory a while ago. There was no one to beat her for salves and potions."

The surname was somewhat familiar to Queenie, being the same as the illustrator of her *Orders of the Fay,* but the crash of thunder made it difficult to converse.

"What do ye mean, the stramash never went awa'?" she managed between peals.

James kissed his fingers. Since he'd just scooped up a dollop of the salve, he grimaced and spluttered, and Queenie laughed. She bent sideways to open a drawer and handed him a clean dishtowel.

The silence resumed. James wiped his face. "I *said*, I cast a glamour of silence, so we could talk," he said. "It wore off."

"Weel, aren't ye fu' o' surprises, bonnie laddie," Queenie said.

James grinned and passed her the dishtowel. "You might want to wipe your face," he said.

"You just want to get me all smeary."

Or does he want me to put my face where he had his? He switched cups wi' me.

He shrugged. "Worth a try." He applied some of the salve to the grazed part of her ankle.

Queenie stiffened, more from fear of potential pain than from pain itself.

He rubbed it in gently and then he slipped her sock off and continued over the top of her foot.

It did hurt, but his hands were gentle.

He could be a doctor . . . a nurse . . . a paramedic . . .

If things were different.

If he had the time.

The second foot was puffy, and it was already beginning to discolour. He treated it as he had the first and then he screwed the lid on the salve. "I'll leave this with you, love. Rub some in a couple of times a day until your feet feel normal." He slid out from underneath and returned her feet to the chair. "You have beautiful feet."

Queenie made a sound of negation. The puffiness and dis-colouration was advancing by the second. Her toes felt like swollen sausages.

"No, you have. A wee bit of temporary damage can't disguise the beautiful proportions of you." He stroked her ankles, running his fingers delicately up to her calves.

"I love curves," he said in wistful tones. Then he changed his tone. "Now, shall we make that Scotch broth?"

Queenie thought about her aborted trip to the city for her costume.

She couldn't hobble about looking for a difficult-to-find shop, and besides, it was presumably pouring out there as well as silent-thundering.

A shadow passed over her heart as she realised she might not have a use for that costume after all.

If she couldn't walk, how could she go to a ball?

Is this a punishment for wanting to see James in a kilt?

"If you like," she said.

"Excellent!" James rubbed his hands like a pantomime villain. He lifted down one of her stew pots and he investigated her fridge. "We can make stock from these chicken legs . . . we'll need mutton and barley, parsnips and carrots and dried peas . . ."

"I haven't got all that," Queenie said, disappointed.

James put the chicken in a small pan and added water and bay leaves.

"Luckily, I have." He washed his hands, kissed his fingers and caught a basin out of the air. "I was making this tonight for my supper." He repeated the action to retrieve a knife and board and then he began a flurry of chopping.

Queenie stared at him.

He was apparently in his element.

He likes cooking? Does Mitch?

106

She had no idea. He *did* cook . . . he'd helped her make cheese tarts. And he certainly loved eating.

She tried to picture Mitch's ecstatic face as he bit into one of her Ruby Tuesday tarts. As usual, she couldn't.

James had things well in hand, so she allowed her attention to wander to the basket on the bench.

"Wha' is that?" she asked.

James glanced at her and then away. "I brought it for you to see," he said.

"But wha' — "

He turned from chopping vegetables, and he lifted the basket into her lap and undid the lid.

Queenie stared at the contents, puzzled.

It wasn't a dog — she had known it couldn't be. However, there was a framed painting of one, an intelligent-looking deerhound with beautiful eyes.

Och, look at you!

Under the painting was a bunch of dried heather tied up with a purple ribbon, and a silver pin with an enamel rose attached to the same ribbon. There was a soft wool blanket in every shade from silver grey to violet to blue, and a knitted bear. There was a pair of soft cords, and a shirt with full sleeves, a smaller version of the argyle sweater James had on, a small pile of dogeared books, a mesh bag of polished stones, some carved driftwood, a soft cloth bag and a tiny carved wooden chest.

The final item was another picture — not a fully worked up painting but a quick sketch. It showed a boy running through a meadow, with a great dog bounding beside him. The artist had caught the boy in profile, glancing down at the dog, which had its muzzle lifted to return the look.

She lifted her gaze in confusion.

"James, what *is* this?"

He turned away and resumed his work on the vegetables.

"Can't you guess, love?"

"No' really."

She could, almost, but if she got it wrong . . .

"It's *me,* my love. This is my childhood — such of it as there was. That's my dear Horace, and a pin I gave to Mistress Emer when she salved one of my hurts . . . her man gave it back to Mum after his lassie went to glory. He's the one who did the pictures for me.

"Most of those are things I loved or used, made, or collected during my *brief candle* time . . . saving only the bear."

Queenie lifted the toy from its nest in the blanket. It was beautifully made, with felt stitched paws, eyes, and smile.

"You never played with this," she said, examining its clean perfection. She pictured her own childhood bear. Her dad had called it *Bearly There* because she'd worn so much of the nap off it with her enthusiasm for taking it everywhere.

James went on, "I never did. It's a hugging toy, you see. Georgie made that for me. She was making some for her own bairns. She said wee Jamie should have memories just as *he* had. It was a kind thought, and so I kept it, but she need not have bothered. How can I have memories of a time when I didn't exist? There never was a wee Jamie. Not in the sense she meant."

Queenie picked up the sketch of the boy and dog. In it, James looked fourteen or so, tall and athletic, but not as broad as the man beside her. His hair was already tied back in the neat style he affected now.

She smiled, but it felt painful, as knowledge came unbidden. Horace was obviously a deerhound — not a breed renowned for longevity — *twelve years? No — possibly eight to ten.*

"Horace was five when Georgie gave him to me," James said. "His master, Georgie's grand-auncle, had gone to glory, and Horace needed someone to love." His knife kept up its steady thudding against the board.

He added, "Look through whatever you like. Read the

books if you want. I'll have to leave when the soup is done, but you can keep those things for as long as you like."

He scraped the mound of vegetables into the larger pot, then turned down the heat under the chicken.

"I'll come back to deal with the stock later. It should really be made ahead."

He threw cubed mutton into the pot.

"Keep those things for as long as you like," he said again. "It's not as though they are of any use to me. Not really." The lid clanged into place. He turned to look down at her feet, avoiding her gaze. "How are your ankles?"

Queenie flexed her feet. Her heart was breaking for him, but there was so little she could do or say. "Ow."

James ran water into the sink, washed knife, board and hands and then kneeled by the side of Queenie's chair. "Will you be all right if I leave you?"

"O' course," she said.

"I could try to find someone to sub for me — maybe Olivier Campania would do it."

"I'm fine." She felt uncomfortable with his close regard. He so obviously wanted to stay.

"I'll need to see you walk before I can leave you," he said.

"And *I'll* need ye to stop with the managing," Queenie responded.

To her surprise, he laughed. "It's not managing . . . I just can't have you crawling about out of misplaced pride and thrawnness. You'll hurt your knees and the broth will spoil."

"Verra weel." She lifted the basket from her lap and set it down gently beside the chair. Then she hitched forwards in the seat and gingerly swung her legs down. She set her feet on the floor and got upright.

Ow.

She grimaced, but although both ankles still felt wrenched and painful, the idea of taking a step was no longer impossible. She took two and wobbled.

James put both arms around her.

She rested against him for a few seconds, feeling the hard, fast thump of his heart.

"You can let go now." Her voice came out cooler than she intended.

He stood back, thrusting his hands into his pockets.

Queenie walked slowly across the kitchen, turned and walked back.

"Weel, Master Stuart?"

He looked at her and then away.

Queenie became aware of the sound of rain on the roof, so the glamour must have worn off for the second time. The thunder and lightning was over.

James moved aside and poked the contents of the pots.

"That broth can simmer a while. I'll turn the chicken off and set it to cool."

He turned and went out of the kitchen abruptly, leaving Queenie open-mouthed behind him.

Chapter Fourteen: Fairings

Queenie Hart, October 25th, 2021

It was five days before Queenie's ankles felt equal to making her expedition to the city.

Her feet cycled from red and swollen to purple and down to yellowish brown. Her plans cycled in similar progression.

Going to the Halloween Ball in costume had seemed such a brilliant idea—James could wear his kilt and enjoy a night out.

Besides, it was her birthday. Why shouldn't she celebrate.

But how can ye . . .

The salve from James's mother was effective, but after the first time, Queenie had to put it on for herself.

James came back to deal with the Scotch broth, but he had a train to meet, and quickly left again.

She wanted to invite him to join her for supper, but he didn't give her the chance.

He telephoned her the next day, and the next, but only to enquire how she was.

He called in briefly with an order and required her to walk for him. She was wearing slippers because she couldn't get into her shoes.

Queenie returned to her baking, and in her down time, she spent hours acquainting herself with the mementos of James's childhood.

There was pitifully little.

Due to the cramped size of the unit at Mother Goose Lane,

she hadn't kept a great many things from her younger days, although she still had Bearly There. She had a wealth of memories instead.

She wanted to take a photograph of James to add to the one she had of Mitch, but apart from that brief visit, he stayed away. Besides, he knew she had the *aide-mémoire*.

Ye dinnae need a photograph o' the bonnie laddie anyway . . . ye ken fine what he looks like.

She had restored the *aide-mémoire* to its frame beside her bed. She refreshed her memory of Mitch's face every morning when she woke and again before she slept.

As soon as she could wear her shoes without too much pain, she made a second attempt to visit the costume shop. She considered riding the tricycle, but in the end, she walked into Fiddle Bay. The bus left at ten, so she set out early, in case she needed to rest on the way.

She had almost reached the post office stop when she fully realised her folly. She was intending to spend a fair amount of money on a costume for a ball . . . but she hadn't yet asked James if he would go with her.

She tried to remember why she'd thought this was a good idea.

To gie him a chance to wear his kilt.

Or to gie you a chance to see him in it.

What a shallow lassie ye are.

Ethel pulled in at the stop just as she reached it, and she steeled herself to get aboard, using the rails to haul herself up the steep steps.

Seeing James at the wheel gave her a pang and her eyes prickled with tears.

She smiled at him, and he smiled back, although he looked puzzled to see her out in public when she'd made such an issue of closeting herself away.

"Sit by me, love," he murmured, and she took the seat across from him.

They couldn't have a private conversation with other passengers nearby, but they managed a brief exchange.

"So, you're feeling better?" he asked.

"Almost healed. Soon be fit for dancing."

"Dancing, is it?"

"Aye—if I hae a guid partner. Will ye gang to the Halloween Ball wi' me, laddie?"

He shot her a sideways glance.

"It's at Oakengrove, on Sunday night."

He said, "Cutting it fine, love. It's my last day."

"Aye, but it would please me weel if ye'd dance wi' me there."

He laughed. "In my dratted kilt, I suppose."

"Ye said ye'd wear it if ye had the occasion."

"I'll wear it anywhere you like in exchange for one kiss."

She said dryly, "No' tradin' fer kisses, laddie. Wear what pleases ye."

"I'll come for you at seven-thirty," he said.

So, he did know about the dance, unless he had guessed the time. She supposed he might read the *Strad*. He certainly knew she did. He'd seen it in her kitchen.

Queenie gave him a quick, uneasy smile. Now she was justified in getting that costume . . . and committed to dancing with James. She only hoped he could dance.

I should hae asked him.

She got down from Ethel at Borrowdale Junction, murmuring, "Thank ye, James," as she left the bus.

Harriet Charming, the woman with the bike, echoed her as she climbed down.

She glanced at Queenie. "I've missed you at the market."

"I'll be back there in a wee while."

"Are you okay, love? I wasn't meaning to eavesdrop, but I heard James ask after your health."

Queenie wondered what else the woman might have heard.

She brazened it out. "I had a wee tumble down some steps, but it's all bonnie noo."

"Good. Speaking of our stand-in driver, what do you think of him? Handsome lad, isn't he."

"Aye, verra," Queenie said.

"And single, I think."

"Aye."

"Something of an enigma, young James —"

"Excuse me, Harriet, I hae to go." Queenie got in the train, glad to see Harriet heading for the other platform. A conversation about James and his romantic status was something she didn't want to have.

Of course the people of Fiddle Bay must find James an enigma. She did, herself.

At Circular Quay, she glanced at the O-Quay Café, wondering what the staff would say if she went in for a coffee. Would they say, "Your usual, Queenie?" Or would she see faces close as they noted the stalker was back in their orbit . . .

Dinnae fash yoursel's. I found my bonnie laddie — or he found me.

She resisted the urge to go in and tell them so. Caledonia was heavy on her mind, and she wanted to get back to the safety of The Belfry as soon as possible.

She looked at the directions she'd had from Nona. That late-night call seemed a long time ago, but fortunately, she'd written down the information.

First, she had to find Lady Lane. She didn't remember ever having been there before, but the area had a bewildering mass of lanes and walkways and she had by no means walked every one of them.

She asked two people, who inexplicably pointed in opposite directions and then fell to arguing. That reminded her of Branok and Gillan disputing over her head back in August. Finally, these two agreed that they must be indicating opposite ends of Lady Lane, which ran parallel to another one whose name they couldn't recall.

Queenie left them to it and consulted her phone. Then she set out hopefully. She took a short cut and a wrong turn and ended up in a shop called *Hebridean Dreams,* which she put down to the Caledonian Fugue. She had picked up a coat of fine Harris tweed and was sliding her arm in to try it on when she jerked herself to order.

She hung the coat back on the rack, noticing the high three-figure price in the collar. It was a beautiful coat, worth every cent, no doubt, but she could not afford distractions — or expensive winter coats.

The assistant eyed her with disapproval. "That's hand-made in Stornoway on the Isle of Lewis. It's a classic piece — an investment."

"Aye, so I see." Queenie nodded to her and backed out of the shop.

"Lassie Lane, Lassie Lane . . ." That wasn't right.

A very young man with fine features glanced at her as she stopped dead, muttering to herself. "Are you looking for Lady Lane, mistress?"

"Aye!" She turned to him gratefully. "I'm all about in ma heid."

"I can show you if you like. Mum works in a shop there."

"Thank ye, bonnie laddie." She closed her mouth before something more inappropriate came out.

He turned back the way he'd come, which suggested she was taking him out of his way, but she was too grateful to demur. She noticed he had slightly pointed ears, but he wasn't wearing silver, so probably was not a pisky.

Mentally, she reviewed her housewarming gift.

Fair skin, slightly pointed ears, delicate features, smiling . . . "Are ye an elf, laddie?" she hazarded.

He gave her a shy look. "Yes, mistress, mostly — at least, I threw that way. My name's Asher."

"Queenie," she said.

He stopped at a narrow lane than might have been no more than a way along the back of a shop. "Lady Lane, Mistress Queenie. What shop were you after?"

"It's called Fairings," she said. She didn't expect a boy — even an elf boy — to frequent ladies' dress shops, but he nodded his comprehension.

"It's on your left. Walk slowly — blink and you'll miss it."

He gave her a shy smile. "Excuse me, but are you the tart lady? Queen of Tarts? I used to buy your tarts at the market for my miss — that is, she's my — "

"Girlfriend?" Queenie asked.

He blushed. "My *lover*," he got out with evident pride.

"More power to yer sporran, then, laddie, an' may ye ever be — " She broke off before she could say something as inappropriate as Oliver Porthwellian at his worst. Hastily, she took a card from her pocket. "I dinnae come to the market here anymore, but if ye're ever in Fiddle Bay, I'm trading there, and I'll be glad to accommodate ye wi' tarts for your lassie."

He grinned. "I might see you there. Jessie loves to be accommodated."

He darted away.

Maybe not so innocent a laddie after all.

Queenie headed down the tiny lane, slowly, as he'd directed, looking to her left. After the incident with the Harris tweed, she didn't dare let herself go on automatic pilot. Her attention paid off when she saw an arch with a swathe of coloured scarves.

Fairings.

She ventured inside and stood looking about with pleasure.

The shop was narrow but deep, with racks of colourful clothes receding towards mirrored doors.

Two women sat behind the counter. One was sewing a collar with tiny invisible stitches, and the other was embroidering.

The older one looked up and smiled. "I'm Jacaranda Fairling, and this is my business partner, Lucida Castleby. How may we help you?"

Queenie had intended to ask for a tartan gown, a sash, and some worsted stockings, but her encounter with the elf lad had given her a new and surely more sensible idea.

"Ma name is Queenie Hart. I'm looking for a wee costume for a Halloween Ball."

The woman, who was appropriately wearing purple, said, "We have some costumes, but we're primarily a dress shop, Ms Hart. We have readymade garments, and we also offer made-to-measure commissions."

"I want a costume for the Queen of Tarts," Queenie said.

She saw incomprehension, and she added, "Verra like the Queen o' Hearts, but tartier. No' something that would give any auld gentlemen heart failure, but..." She described curves in the air.

"Something to make the most of your assets," Jacaranda Fairling said.

"Aye. Let's face it—I'm big and strawberry blonde and buxom."

The woman tilted her head and laid down her sewing. "You say that as if it's a bad thing."

"No' at all!" Queenie said, startled. She'd come to realise Lassie Haggis *loved* her curves.

"I'm glad you see that... at Fairings we encourage folk to play to their strengths."

"Aye." She looked around at the dresses hanging on long rails.

The woman considered her. "You're not twins, are you?" she asked abruptly.

Queenie's thoughts flew to James and Mitch. They weren't twins, but two men inextricably linked by an accident of birth.

"No, of course you're not," the woman answered herself.

"Only child," Queenie murmured.

"What do you think, Lu?" The woman glanced at her partner, a slight, vague-looking woman with soft brown hair, a pointed chin and eyes at once dreamy and startled.

Lu looked momentarily at Queenie and gave the tiniest nod.

Jacaranda said, "I expect we could manage that."

This was welcome news, but then came the less welcome intelligence that the costume would need to be made up from scratch and wouldn't be ready until late on the Friday afternoon before Halloween.

Queenie supposed that was more than she could expect . . . but it meant another trip to the city. She wished she had a fully briefed girlfriend who would come with her for moral support and do the talking for her.

Dellion Tredennick's face came to mind. Dellion knew her and seemed to like her, but the thought was ridiculous. She and Andy lived hours away, down in Victoria. Gillan — no, that would be an imposition. Gillan wasn't a friend, but a distant cousin's wife, of another generation. Nona, although friendly, wasn't briefed and she wasn't exactly a *friend*. Besides, she was always busy. Willow Dee? Another imposition.

I'd love to meet Georgiana . . . I'm sure she'd come with me.

James had told her quite a bit about his cousin. He seemed very fond of her.

The woman in purple was waiting for an answer, so she said, lamely, "That's cutting it a wee bit fine."

She seemed to hear James saying the same thing about the Halloween Ball.

"It's the best I can do, Ms Hart. Until then I'll be elbow-deep in black crepe."

The implication was that she should have come in earlier.

So I would hae, if I'd no' taken my wee tumble down the stairs.

The conversation plunged into odd uncharted byways

then, including an odd story about a Christmas tree doll and then segueing into a discussion on fairies.

Queenie had by then realised that one or probably both of the Fairings ladies were fay, so she felt it safe to ask obliquely if the costume she had ordered might include a wee bit of magic. She didn't phrase it that way, but it seemed they understood her well enough.

She felt she was so far down the rabbit hole by now that she might never climb out, so she made her escape.

"Namaste." She put her palms together and bent her head for a moment.

It was only later, as she sat in the train heading back to Borrowdale Junction, that she realised why the ladies had looked so nonplussed. She'd meant to use the fay farewell Andy employed but instead she'd come out with a Hindu greeting.

I hope I'm no' aboot to manifest an Indian swami.

At least she hadn't called the women anything unfortunate in cod Scots . . . as far as she could remember.

When she disembarked at the junction, Ethel was waiting.

Queenie got in and paid her fare and then, without waiting for an invitation, she took the seat nearest the driver.

"Greet you, James."

"And you, Queenie," he said. "Where have you been?"

None o' your business, she thought, but then she changed her mind. It *was* his business, in a way. She said, "I've been to find oot aboot a costume for the Halloween Ball. I've put in ma order, so I hope you're still up for it, laddie."

"I'm up for anything to be with you," he said.

To Queenie's surprised embarrassment this announcement brough forth a titter and a patter of applause from behind them.

She glanced back, biting her tongue to keep from uttering an expletive in lassie haggis.

"There's a surprise," one old woman remarked. "I thought you had your eye on our Mitch, love."

119

"An' *I* thought auld besoms were apt to be deif as posts!" Queenie snapped.

That brought another murmur of applause and Queenie wanted to sink through the floor.

"I'm so sorry," she muttered.

"That's all right, love," another passenger said. "Kez was just having a dig at you. She's a bit Mitch's way, aren't you Kez?"

"I wouldn't kick him out of my bed on a cold night," the unrepentant Kez said cheerfully. "In fact, I couldn't, what with my arthritis and all." She added, "Saving your pardon, James—I suppose that's kiboshed any chance I had of a lift to my door? Just so you know, I wouldn't kick *you* out in the snow either. You and Mitch ought to come with a government health warning."

"I'll take you to your door—and save you a dance at the Halloween Ball," James said.

Kez cackled and said it would need to be a short one and that he mustn't tell Mitch.

James promised he wouldn't, which Queenie thought was at least technically true.

"Make sure you come to claim your dance before the witching hour, Kez," he added.

"Why, love? Do you turn into a pumpkin?"

"Something like that," James said.

One by one, the passengers disembarked, and Queenie wondered what would happen when it was her turn.

The last time Mitch had offered her a full ride home, she'd snapped at him.

She didn't want to snub James, especially since he'd agreed to go to the ball with her, but according to James, Mitch would know exactly what had passed between Queenie and his alter ego. If she said *aye* to James's offer when she'd turned Mitch's down—

Och, Black Sneck fly away with it! He's been in ma hoosie making

Scotch broth, aye, an' given me a wee window into his soul . . . carried me to the kitchen, got me hot in the coochie by stroking ma feet . . . so why make such a havering over a ride home in his bus?

She knew why, of course. Ethel was Mitch's bus. He was the real driver. This was *his* job. James was the substitute, the ring-in, the stand-in, the man with fractured memories and a short life full of questions no one could answer.

An enigma, Harriet Charming had called him.

Ye dinnae know the half o' it, hen.

Ethel pulled in at the post office, and Queenie made a motion to get up.

She was the last passenger to disembark, and James got out of his seat and moved quickly around to the passenger side.

He held out his arms. "I'll help you down, my love."

"I can manage."

"If we're going to dance the night away at the Halloween Ball, I need to practise holding you in my arms so I don't explode on the dance floor. Also, I can't have you falling out of the bus."

"That would be a bad idea," she agreed.

"Which? Letting me hold you in my arms, exploding on the floor, or falling out of the bus?"

"All of them."

His face shuttered, and he dropped his arms, backing away.

Queenie's heart gave a great thump.

"Och, take nae notice o' me," she said wearily. She let go of the edge of the door and reached for him.

James stepped up again and lifted her gently down. "My love," he murmured. She felt him put his cheek on her hair for a fleeting second and then he stepped aside.

"Shall I see you before Sunday?" he asked.

"Aye, on Friday. I hae to go doon to the city to fetch my wee costume then."

He nodded and then he got back into the bus.

Chapter Fifteen: Conversation with Dellion

Queenie Hart, October, 2021

Back at The Belfry, with the bats rustling away in the belltower, Queenie made herself tea and sat at her table to mope.

James's situation was so unfair. She'd refused him so much as a kiss and he knew perfectly well she'd been to bed with Mitch. Mitch hadn't needed to ask. She'd offered.

Her head ached as she tried to think of the right thing to do. She was committed to going with him to the Halloween Ball, but the thought of what awaited him after that made her miserable.

She wanted to offer him something . . . some hope, or compensation.

She remembered the first time he'd asked her for a kiss. *Just for me.*

I should hae given it to him. What harm could it do?

There was just one person she felt she could ask for advice on the matter.

"Greet you, Queenie."

"Andy." She got to the point. "Could I hae a wee word with Dellion?"

"I expect so—as long as you're not plotting mayhem or planning to talk about me in embarrassing detail."

"No."

She heard him call his wife's name.

"She's coming as soon as she's untangled the lads."

"Thanks. And Andy—could I hae this wee word in private?"

"Of course, lovie," he said easily. "I'll have her take the phone out into the sunshine."

"Thank you." Her voice broke.

"Are you all right, Queenie?"

"Aye."

To her relief, he took her word for it.

After a while, Dellion came on the line. "What's up, sweet? Andy said you needed a quiet word, so I'm out in the garden . . . He's promised to keep the boys and Oliver under control, so we won't be disturbed. The rest of the partners won't come out here."

"The rest?"

"Oh, yes. You didn't think it was just Oliver and Andy and me, did you? There *must* be at least one Porthwellian and one Tredennick in the firm, and when I married Andy, that left the Porthwellians thin on the ground. Oliver was already eighty-nine . . . Granddad is a silversmith, and Dad and my uncles—well, they do other things. Luckily, my little brother Trevik came in with us—not a partner yet, but he will be—and Andy's dad—but, as Andy did say once, you don't need to know all that. What can I do for you, sweet?"

Queenie took a deep breath and crushed down Caledonia. "I need a wee bit—some more advice."

"About horizontal dessert?" There was curiosity in Dellion's voice.

"Not exactly, but—I don't know if you can help, but I've got myself into one of those situations where I don't know the *right* thing to do."

"Go ahead," Dellion said. "I might not be able to advise you, but I'll listen. Is it about the raincheck man, or the handsome laddie you had with you the other morning when you called to talk with Oliver?"

"Both, in a way. Do you remember I mentioned a person who had another self who is a spaniel?"

"Yes—a pisky. But isn't the raincheck man a fix-it pixie? I'm sure he is."

"Aye. Weel, it turns oot—" She jerked herself back into line. "Mitch, my horizontal raincheck man, *is* a pixie, but he has another self too. I didnae—didn't know until I called him to come and deal with the bats in ma belfry—"

"And that other self is the laddie who was with you when you wiped the floor with Oliver," Dellion concluded.

"Aye. James Stuart."

"He seemed very stable for a mani-man," Dellion said.

"If you mean real—aye, he is."

"He's a braesider."

"Aye."

"And handsome. Almost as fine to look at as my Andy. And he has his eye on you all right. So where's the problem?"

"He has only one month a year to *be*. I met him last October, and I turned him down. I was sorry right away, but I couldnae find him again—and then I met Mitch and we . . . had horizontal dessert. Then we quarrelled. It was mostly my fault."

Dellion didn't demur at that, but then, she had heard Queenie in full flow when she tore some verbal strips off Oliver.

"When the bats bothered me, I called Mitch to help, but when he arrived, he was James." Queenie broke off, wondering anxiously if Dellion could even halfway understand that.

She underestimated the pisky woman, because Dellion said, "I see. And of course you recognised him as the man you met and lost last year."

"Aye."

"And so you have two handsome men, and they *both* have

a fancy for bedding the Queen of Tarts."

"Aye."

"It's not surprising, sweet. You're a fine figure of a woman, and I'm sure you're a happy and generous lover. Cuddly and quick to light up—I can see that. Andy thinks so too."

"He does?"

"Oh, yes. He told me so. No waiting around while she takes her time with that one . . ."

"Don't you mind?"

"Why would I mind? *I'm* the one who gets to be his miss, and his forever lover, and the mother of his little lads. I'm glad he told me he finds you sexy, because if he'd denied it, I'd have thought he was fibbing, or losing his edge. There's nothing so hard to handle as a married man who's gone smug and settled and lost his edge. I *want* him to appreciate beautiful things—so long as he does it with his eyes and not his hands or his willy." She gave a naughty giggle and then she composed herself. "To get back to you—both aspects of your man want you, so, I repeat, what's the problem? It would surely be far worse if one of them was hot for someone else."

"Mitch is a fix-it pixie, remember."

"Oh yes." Dellion was quiet for a few seconds and then she said, "Of course, I don't know your Mitch, but I've met a couple of others of that type. One of them runs a garage repair shop down near Patterdale, not far from where we are. He's an exceedingly *odd* person—the greenest pixie I've ever met. He looks about sixteen, but he's a man all right. Any car he can't fix can't be fixed by anyone, ever, and his wife has *that* look . . .the look of a woman who gets laid hot and hard, thoroughly and often and who can't *wait* to do it again."

She paused again and then she went on, "As I've said before, pixies are lovely folk, but the men are jealous as hell. Not the way humans are . . . no pixie man will ever try to control his miss—she'd nail his balls to the door if he did—but if they feel their dear darling might be smiling at some other lucky man with more than seemly warmth, they go *green* . . . That shames them and then they sink into a misery so deep it hurts to look at them. Occasionally, they just die."

This was not what Queenie wanted to hear.

"I'm no' Mitch's girlfriend . . . or his dear darling," she ventured.

"What are you, then?" Dellion sounded genuinely curious.

"I think he loves me . . . in a way. I'm sure he does. Rain-checks and all. He says he'd do anything for me, but then— he wants to *fix* things for everyone." She thought she wasn't doing Mitch justice, but the way they'd parted depressed her. She said, miserably, "I wish I'd been nicer to him. I miss him."

"So what are you asking, exactly, sweet?" Dellion asked gently.

"James has just one month a year—October. He can't have a proper fulltime job. He can't have normal friendships . . . he certainly can't have a family or a wife or a home of his own. He can't even have a d-dog to love, unless someone else keeps it for most of the time. He can't have summer, or Christmas or even Burns Night. It's so *cruel*."

"It sounds so, but there's a good chance he's contented with what he has. I know of a few mani-folk, and they timeshare happily with the main selves. Though to be sure they're a bit less solid than your James seems to be. More like—I don't know—fairy-tale characters. Larger than life. Flamboyant. They live life to the full, but in short bursts. Up like a rocket and then down to earth to dissolve back into their main selves. If they were about consistently for years at a time, I think they'd burn out. They're not *meant* to be viable for sustained periods."

"James feels short-changed, though. He met me first, you see, and he gave me a wish. I had nothing I could properly wish for, so I wished for him to be lucky and loved—"

"Oh . . . *criminy!*" Dellion said in tones of foreboding. "You've got a wish-match on your hands. Oh, Queenie . . ."

"Is tha' so bad?"

"No—not *bad,*" Dellion said unconvincingly. She added, "Unwise, maybe."

"I didnae know!"

"How could you? But you see, sweet, he gave you a wish. You didn't refuse it. You accepted it, and then you turned it about and *used it for him.* It can be done, but the poor laddie fell head over sporran for you. And then you got mixed up with his other self—"

Queenie said, in a small voice, "If there were a way I could hae the twa together to talk it oot . . ."

"That's not an option, sweet. They can't ever exist at the same time. It's like—oh, think of a looking glass. Think of standing before it. There's your reflection, smiling back at you. But, if you step away to the side, or behind the glass, your reflection isn't there. It can't step out of the glass to stand side by side with you."

"But Mitch and James are no' reflections," Queenie said, puzzled.

"No. It wasn't meant to be an exact analogy. It was meant to show the impossibility of the thing. It's a pity you didn't work out where you stood with your horizontal pixie man before the laddie turned up again. I noticed you say the pixie man's name first—Mitch and James—so it might be safer and kinder if you can stay out of the laddie's range. There are just a few more days before your pixie is back and you can make your apologies and take him to bed. Don't see the laddie again, or you'll get more muddled."

"I invited him to the Halloween Ball. He should have *some* fun, and it's my birthday. And . . ." She stopped, not wanting to admit to her selfish desires.

"And what?"

"And I hae the need to see him in a kilt—"

"I see. I'm sure he'd look fantabulous in a kilt. I also see you can't *un*invite him. Too cruel to let him down. You'll have to play it by ear. Just don't do anything you will need to lie about later. Pixies don't like that. They *really* don't like it. A pisky man might stretch a point for a little prevarication because he'll be wanting to do it himself one day, but a pixie man—never. He'd never forgive you for the lie, and he'd never forgive himself for putting you in the situation where you felt you needed to lie."

"I couldnae lie anyway . . . they both remember what the other one does."

"I see. They're not *completely* separate then." Dellion was silent for a good fifteen seconds. Then she said, more cheerfully, "That could be a good thing, actually. You won't have to waste hours debriefing each one when his turn in the driving seat comes around. If you get past Halloween unscathed, I suggest you have a proper, honest talk with your pixie man. Find out if he wants you for keeps."

"I hadnae thought that far! We were only just beginning and remember, we quarrelled."

"If he wants you at all, I mean, if he began with you at all, he probably wants to keep you . . .or have you keep him. Unless they're having a friendly with a miss who knows the score, pixies generally don't start what they don't intend to continue. They're too scared of falling into soul cold when it ends. If he considers himself yours—"

"Then I'll hae to promise to stay awa' from James." A pang went through Queenie at the thought.

"No! Three-hundred-and-thirty-four times no! As you said, that would be cruel to a laddie who can't have very much of his own. If your pixie man loves you and intends to be yours—and if you agree to have him, and you make up your mind *not* to push him away again, then you'll have a devoted man to love you forever. He'll just have to accept that for one month of the year you will be delighting the loins and lighting the life of another equally loving and deserving man. It's not going to be simple, but as far as I can see, it's the only viable option—unless you want to toss them both out of your bed and out of your life forever. If so, you'd better do it as soon as possible before anything *really* unfortunate happens."

Queenie relaxed. What Dellion had told her felt right. It *was* right. Now she had to work out how to settle things with her men.

Could she truly have them both? It sounded greedy, but what if the greedy option was the best one for them all?

She bade Dellion a grateful farewell.

Right on cue, the bats in the belltower set up a great chittering and squeaking, so Queenie marched down to the narthex. She took off her shoe and she banged it hard against the closed door.

"Stop yer stramash, ye clettering beasties, or I'll lay ma tawse against yer furry bahoochies!"

The bats stopped.

Chapter Sixteen: Friday

Queenie Hart, October 29th, 2021

On Friday afternoon, two days before Halloween, Queenie walked to the bus stop.

She mounted the steep steps into Ethel, and she sat down in the seat nearest to James.

She looked at him with a hopeful and proprietary interest.

I could love ye – give ye kisses, all for ye.

"I'm awa' to fetch ma wee costume," she said.

He nodded.

"When I'm back, I'd like it fine if you would take supper wi' me at The Belfry."

His eyes lit up with painful eagerness.

"Just supper, bonnie laddie," she said gently.

"I'll be glad of anything I'm allowed to have," he murmured.

Queenie should have felt generous, having offered James something he wanted, but instead she felt uncomfortable — as if she were playing games with his emotions.

It's no' like that . . . Does a mun who is hungry not want a buttermilk tattie if he cannae hae the whole roast dinner? And maybe it will come out right for us all.

She made it to Fairings with no more than three wrong turnings. This time, no sweet-faced elf lad offered to guide her, and she missed the turn into Lady Lane. On the plus side, she didn't detour into Hebridean Dreams and had no urge to pay too much for Harris tweed. On the minus side, she did have to take a quick about turn when she found herself yearning over a tray of Georgian silver kilt pins in an antique shop. She had got as far as asking the proprietor to unlock the cabinet when she caught sight of her reflection in the glass, along with the reflection of the grandfather clock behind her. It was five minutes to five.

"Och, there, but I'm late for an appointment," she said regretfully, and she got out with her funds and her dignity intact.

She made it to Fairings just at closing time.

Jacaranda Fairling smiled at her without any trace of impatience at having to delay locking up. "Greet you, Queen of Tarts."

"And ye." Queenie looked about for the fawn-eyed woman, but Jacaranda was alone.

"Lu has gone home to her man — they're having dinner with their son and his girl."

Jacaranda took a parcel from under the counter and set it down before Queenie. "Here you are, my lassie. One Queen of Tarts costume, as requested. It's short, it's startling and it's magnificent. Do you have opaque tights to wear?"

"Aye, blue ones, made o' guid Scottish wool." Queenie, glad she had kept this relic of a former Caledonian-inspired spending spree, tugged at the paper, but the woman held up a hand to stop her.

"Wait, please."

"Aye?"

The dressmaker looked at her kindly. "I'm unsure what's going on with you, Queen of Tarts. I'm not trying to insult you, but there's something odd about you."

"Aye, that would be the Caledonian Curse. A wee Halloween manifestation that lasts through October and sometimes leaks backwards into September," Queenie said. "It isnae harmful, but it can be a right pain in the bahoochie. Expensive too, but I believe I have solved *that* wee problem."

"I don't pretend to understand that. I consider I'm good at reading folk, but my friend Lucida is much better. She wanted you to have exactly what you asked for, so here it is. It's not just a bundle of cloth, though, and I can't in all conscience let you go off without giving you a bit of advice. Or maybe a warning is a better way to put it."

Queenie said, "You're fay."

"Yes. I'm an elf maid. You need not fear angles or traps with me, because I don't seek them, and I don't set them. I want folk to have what they desire . . . a dress to make them feel beautiful and true to themselves. That is, with the proviso that it will do no harm to anyone else."

Queenie inclined her head. "How could a dress do harm, hen?"

"Usually, I can tell if what someone wants to have might cause damage. For example, if a young woman came in and asked me for a gown that will turn a man's heart to her, I'd want to be sure that man didn't owe his allegiance to someone else. I'd also not want to make a dress that would give the wrong impression. If a pisky minx asked for a gown to make her seem simple and childlike, I would have to say no. Such a gown would be deceptive. In your case, I'm not sure. You wanted a dress to please a man—"

"Aye. But he doesnae belong to anyone else."

"Then why are you troubled?"

Queenie considered spilling the whole tale, but it was getting late, and she had already made up her mind what to do. "I hae it in my mind no' to tell ye . . . but I mean nae harm to him, or to anyone else. My hand on it."

She offered her hand, and the elf woman took it.

"I believe you." The woman gave her a long look and released her hand. "Take your costume and enjoy it . . . but don't put it on until you're ready to wear it for real."

"But it may no' fit!"

"It will fit. It will look magnificent on you. You will be the most yourself that you have ever been." The woman's face dissolved into a grin. "And I must say it was a treat to work on something that *didn't* call for metres of black crepe. Red and gold brocade and velvet — so delightful. You will be the belle of the ball."

Queenie tucked the package under her arm. "How much do I owe ye?"

Jacaranda jotted down some figures, adding them swiftly. The she turned to Queenie and gave her the price.

After her difficulty with trying to get a price out of Mitchell for moving her and her chattels from Mother Goose Lane to The Belfry, this transaction was as smooth as silk and as transparent as water. It was a high price, as it must be when using embroidered brocade and high-sheen velvet, but surprisingly not so high as the Harris tweed or a Georgian pin would have been. She took her purse from her pocket and handed over some notes. "Thank ye."

"Have a lovely time at the ball, and may the night bring whatever good things you deserve," the woman said.

"*Nos da.*" Queenie left the shop. She wasn't too sure what to make of that parting comment.

Nor was she sure why Jacaranda Fairling had looked startled when she said goodbye.

She caught the train by the skin of her teeth, and she spent the journey waiting with trepidation for her supper with James. She hoped she hadn't made a misjudgement in inviting him.

She'd made it clear it was for supper alone, but had he taken that in? Was it fair?

"You got your costume?" he asked as she boarded Ethel.

"Aye."

Other people boarding took his attention, and Queenie was

glad. The light in his loch-grey eyes when he looked at her did peculiar things to her insides.

She stayed on board after the last passenger had been dropped at Oakengrove, and James turned off into October Road.

"Odd, that a lassie with a Halloween manifest should live in October Road," he said.

"Aye, and at number thirty-one . . ." She added, "I keep meaning to ask someone—maybe Bernie or Maureen Tucker—if The Belfry is number thirty-one, where the diel are the other hoosies?"

She didn't expect him to answer, but he said, "This road is a symptom of a forecast that failed. Fiddle Bay was settled at a time when the mainstay of travel was by horse and carriage. The church was built with the expectation that the town would grow, with houses right through and beyond, but the age of the motor car came along and the distance to Sydney was suddenly not so great. The bay never reached its expected potential in the population stakes."

"How did ye—" She broke off.

"How did a part-time man know that?" He glanced across at her. "I read a lot. There's not a lot else to do in my free time. Free time being what is not used up by keeping seats warm for *him*. Also, he knows, and so, by extension, do I. It's a surprisingly common phenomenon."

"I see." She perceived he meant the town that failed to grow rather than his own situation, which must be peculiarly uncommon, even among fay.

"You don't like when I denigrate *him*, do you."

"I do not. He doesnae . . ." She saw the trap before her feet.

"He doesn't denigrate me. That's because he doesn't mention me at all, or even think of me, if he can possibly avoid it," he said dryly.

Obviously not.

The bus pulled smoothly into Kirk Circle and swished to a

stop by The Belfry.

"How are your rackety lodgers?" he asked in a lighter tone.

"Rackety."

"You'll be shut of them in a few days."

"Until next October, I expect," she said. She was sure Oliver would have made provision for bats-in-the-belfry-revisited. A little thing such as his tenant's convenience wouldn't sway him from his agenda.

James stepped down from the bus, making it around to the passenger side before Queenie could disembark. He held out his hands to her. "Remember, I have a vested reason for wanting you *not* to fall down any more steps."

After a small hesitation, she wedged her parcel under her arm and accepted his help. "You smell of shortbread," he said in her ear.

"I'm a pastrycook. It—"

"Goes with the job," he said. "Just like flour on the chest. I remember."

Queenie remembered, too.

She gently disengaged and went to the door. She was far from sure this was a good idea, but she was determined to get through the maze of ethical conundrums with the best grace she could.

She *had* wished for James to have luck and love . . .

Dellion thought it might work.

She gestured for James to go in ahead of her while she applied her ear to the warded door. A fluttering thump greeted her.

"The beasties are wearing hobnailed boots," she commented, thumping back with her fist. "Wheest, ye *sìthiche ialt!*"

"What?" James asked, but Queenie shook her head. She had no idea what she meant by that.

It was early for supper, but she decided to make a start.

"What would ye like to eat?"

"Potatoes," he said unexpectedly.

"Really? Not Scotch broth?"

"Do you have any?"

"No."

"I also like eggs. And oats."

Queenie felt a surge of delight. "I can accommodate *all* those likes, laddie. How do potato pancakes sound?"

"With cheese?"

"With cheese."

"I'll grate the cheese."

She handed him cheese and the small grater and then she used the larger one to grate a pile of potatoes.

She covered the white mound with cheesecloth and pressed down.

"There are salad things in the fridge," she said, as she whisked eggs with black pepper and parsley and a drop of milk.

James assembled a salad while she mixed in the potato and fine oatmeal, heated the pan to smoking and started frying the pancakes.

"Not just a pastrycook," he said.

"O' course not! Did ye suppose I ate nothing but tarts?"

"Well, love, I know you eat Scotch broth. Er—you *did* eat it? You didn't pour it away down the end of the garden for fear I'd inserted something underhanded?"

"I ate it," she said. *And I thought of you with every spoonful.*

They sat down to supper in the kitchen, and Queenie raised one of the subjects she'd wanted to air.

"What do you like doing?"

"Is that a trick question?" he asked.

"No. I mean it. What do you enjoy doing, aside from reading and cooking? I know you must have liked carving when you were younger, but there wasn't very much else in your wee basket o' memories to show what you like doing *now*."

He seemed nonplussed. "I like to watch folk down at the quay. I have coffee there. Sometimes I pretend I'm a tourist, and that I fly home on the last day of the month. That accounts for me not being *available* for later meet-ups."

"Do you pick up lassies?"

His fair skin went a dull plum red.

"Why wouldn't you?" she said gently. "You can't meet them through work, or friends, and you obviously have needs."

He looked uncomfortable, so she moved on. "You spend time with your cousin and her family, and with your parents."

"Sometimes. Not so often nowadays. The nievies are growing up, and soon they'll not be so happy to play with Auncle Jamie. Already their interests are changing too fast for me to keep up with."

"You dinnae—travel? Paint? Write? Play sport?"

He shrugged. "Where would I go, and with what? I have to do the driving and deliveries."

"But *why*?"

He seemed puzzled.

"I understand you do some of the work Mitch does, so he can keep his job when he's—unavailable, but *why*? Why should *you* be his fill-in?"

"Who else?"

"Cannae he get someone? Olivier, maybe?"

"Olivier has his own work . . . though he'd stand in for an emergency. No, I'm stuck with it."

"*I* would do it, to give you time for yourself."

He put down his fork and stared at her.

"Why no'? Lassies can be drivers." She added, "I don't have a bus licence, but I could get one, maybe. You should have more time."

James laughed, but it wasn't a happy sound. "Time for what? Nothing I do can lead anywhere. As you say, I can pick up a lassie . . . or a miss . . . or even a human woman. I can woo her and make her laugh. She'll be happy in my bed — but it's really *his* bed unless we go to her place. Most women don't want a stranger to know where they live."

Queenie bit her lip, remembering her hesitancy to let Mitch know she was spending those first nights alone in The Belfry.

"I can never be with a woman for more than a few weeks, and then I'm gone. I can't marry her or promise her forever. Even if I did, how could I expect any woman to wait eleven months for me . . .even a fay one who knows the score? I can't park a lover with Georgiana the way I used to leave dear old Horace. It would be unfair, even if she should agree. And if I bring a woman to my bed — to *his* bed — what if she comes back on a whim and finds *him*? Is he going to explain to her about me and offer himself as a substitute? He can't even bring himself to speak my name to *you!*"

"I see that." She sat looking at him. He was so precisely her type. She was no fan of resentment or of self-pity, but she understood he had few options available to him. She supposed Mitch had a much milder version of the same problem . . . more like her own. None of them could function smoothly through a whole twelve months, but at least she and Mitch had *most* of a year to be themselves and to further any relationship.

If we'd only met last November . . . if we'd had months together, I would have told him about Caledonia Calling, and he would have told me about James . . . Would he not?

"Are there many people like you?" she asked, trying another approach.

"Scrap-and-tatter people? Part-time folk?"

"Manifestation selves." Gillan St Ives had told her about piskies, but James wasn't one of them.

"Quite a number," he said. "A lot of courtfolk have them,

braesiders—the men, anyway. My great-grandfather was one of them. Some hobs . . ."

"What do *they* do?"

"Pop up for a couple of days a year, if they're seasonal, or phase in and out at will if not. That's what most of them do. I'm the only one any of my family knows about who is *persistent, regular, seasonal* and *stable* and . . . dammit . . . *ordinary*."

"You'll need to explain those terms in context. They sound like types of ghosts."

"That's one thing I'm not. I'm corporeal. Let's see. *Persistent* means I'm me, *not* him, for extended and unbroken periods. I can't summon him, or hand over to him, and neither can he do it for me—not that he would. He'd far rather not have me at all.

"*Regular* means I'm a repeating pattern that can be accurately forecast. On October the first, there I'll be. On November the first, there *he'll* be.

"*Seasonal* means I'm tied to a seasonal event—Halloween—just as you are.

"*Stable* means I'm immutable. I'm stuck in this form, and I will always look this way, although obviously I age along with *him*. My hair will be this colour until it turns to grey. When he's an old pixie man, I'll be an auld laddie. When he goes to glory, so will I—I think. Maybe I'll simply evaporate. Some of the courtfolk mani-men can generate clothing, or longer hair, or another eye colour—and some braemen sprout beards they couldn't grow when they're in main-self form, and they appear in great kilts and fearsome sporrans, tattoos or woad. You name it, there are mani-selves out there that can do it. Only not me." He sighed, sounding more frustrated than self-pitying.

"*Ordinary* means what you think it does. I'm just like any other man of my order and age, except that I'm not around for eleven months of the year." He looked her in the eye. "The day you met me . . . once I got rid of the statue costume, which, by the way, was a glamour . . . you took me for a normal person, didn't you? Human, even?"

"Aye. I thought you verra good-looking, and maybe a tourist."

"If you met a manifested courtfolk man, you *wouldn't* think he was a tourist. You'd think he'd wandered out of a theatre, or off a movie set, or through a magic portal from the days of chivalry. If you met a manifested braeman, you might think you'd arrived at a re-enactment of the Battle of Culloden, and you might want to run for your life before he lit up to squalling on his pipes or prancing about with a sgian-dubh or crossed swords or howling about in woad. He'd do it, too. To prance and squall and howl is written in whatever passes for his DNA."

"I like the pipes."

"Of course you do. You'd love to get your hands on a manifested braeman. You'd have him down in the heather with his kilt flipped up and he'd be blaring like a stag in no time as he shot his bolt."

Queenie just managed not to snap at him. She knew it was hurt and frustration making him speak that way.

"Why haven't I noticed those folk, if there are so many of them around?"

He lifted one shoulder and he said dryly, "They're seasonal, *brief candle* folk, and the main selves mostly make sure they manifest *over there*. The human realm isn't a good setting for mani-folk. They make humans doubt their sanity."

"Then why don't *you* stay *over there*?"

"Because *he* lives here, where he can *fix* easily. And because I can *pass*, as we put it, far more easily than just about any other mani-man or maid. Besides, I'm just as much an object of pity *over there* as I am here — more so."

"But surely they understand better *over there*?"

"Oh yes, they understand all too well. The water maids and tree maids and the other delightful maids who tend to the lonely boys know exactly what I am. *Poor Laddie Sometimes,* they call me, and they offer me their arms and their mossy banks as a kindness. And when I return to those maids as the next October rolls around, they barely recall my name—or else they're wed to some fortunate man and swelling with his child. Sometimes they've even cradled his babe already, and they offer to let me hold it out of kindness."

Queenie got up to turn on the jug. She knew she was playing for time. Nothing she'd thought of so far seemed workable . . . other than the one big toss of the dice that Dellion had recommended, and that would depend largely on Mitch. Surely she *must* work things out with Mitch before she put any proposal to James. It would be cruel to offer him something she might never be able to deliver.

She made tea, and she sat down again.

Then, she held out both hands across the table, palms up.

" Are we having a séance? Or an exorcism? You cannot banish me, dearie. I can't be banished. I can't just evaporate while *he* lives, and I wouldn't if I could."

"Noo, ye drompkin fuzzbaw!" She screwed up her face and then she tried again. "We're no' having a séance. It might disturb the beasties in the belltower. If ye're no' wishfu' to take my hands, say so."

He took her hands. "I'm sorry, Queenie. I don't know why I'm acting like this. My time's getting short, and instead of making you uncomfortable with my self-pitying yowls, I should be enjoying every moment I have with you."

"Even if I call ye dreadfu' names?"

"Even so. At least I know I'm making an impression. And it's fun to hear you spout forth—so long as you don't imply *he* is my spaniel bitch—or that I am his. For some reason that is a step too far."

"Verra weel. I had a wee talk with Dellion Tredennick."

He lifted his chin. "How did you keep the bat-enabling old man quiet while you did that?"

"Andy had him under control. I asked Dellion a few things about you and Mitch. Don't be offended, please. I'm new to manifestations—never heard the term until a couple o' months ago. In fact, I'm new to fay people. Dellion has met you, in the manner of speaking, and she knows about Mitch, although she's never met him."

"So, what had the delightful pisky miss to say about us?"

"She *is* delightful, isn't she?"

"Yes," James said frankly. "Master Tredennick is a lucky man."

"She's probably nicer than I am."

He squeezed her hands gently. "Don't fish, dearest. I wouldn't trade a dozen delightful pisky misses for one glorious Queen of Tarts."

Queenie went on in a hurry, "She had a few helpful things to say, and one was that it was a pity I hadn't had that long talk with Mitch before *you* showed up again. We planned to, but first I overslept and then I went into a stupid huff and railed at him, and I wouldn't let him bring me hame. The fact is, I know your view o' him, but not his o' you."

"That's because he doesn't admit to my existence. Even to himself, probably."

"Weel, now I know aboot ye he cannae—can't pretend you don't exist. He'll have no excuse to."

"I don't think he'll want to discuss me, however. He never does. If Mum and Dad, or the sistren or even Georgie start to mention me, he switches off. Even when he's making his provision for my return, he can't bring himself to do any more than change his *available* note on the website to *unavailable during October*."

"Oh, Lord! It's Dad and Branok over again!"

"I beg your pardon?"

"My dad's human, but he has a kind of cousin called Branok St Ives . . . the pisky halfling man who helped me qualify for The Belfry. Dad's a good man, and a lovely dad, but he's a few years older than Branok and they just don't get along. They never did. There's no proper reason why they don't like one another . . . Dad admits it's mostly on his side, but Branok — never mind. It seems to me that you and Mitch are both lovely guys wi' a lot to offer, if you'd just stop resenting one another."

"We don't not get on. We've never met," James pointed out.

"Dad and Branok never meet if they can help it. The last time was at a wedding, and the icicles were verra palpable. They were *polite*."

"*We* don't have a choice in the matter. We *can't* meet."

"No. But you know what happens in his life. You don't spend eleven months of the year in a coma. What *do* you do in your — downtime?"

"When not on-stage? I live at one remove. It's as if I'm experiencing things second-hand, so I'm aware of them but not — not in the driver's seat. I'm a passenger. I can't choose to do things or choose not to. I can't follow my inclinations. I can't prevent him from following his." He faltered. "I'll give you an example, although you might not like it. A while ago *he* met a widow. She was in a world of pain, so he had the imperative to fix it. He couldn't give her what she wanted, which was her own life with her husband back, but he found a way to take the edge off her pain until she could move on. When she was somewhat healed, he even found a likely man for her pleasure and convenience . . . although that was no picnic in the park."

Queenie nodded soberly. "He told me about that."

"I know. I remember. But he didn't tell you her name, or

how she looked, or the way her skin felt, or how it was when her tears poured over his shoulder, and she cried for her loss while he was *in* her and sobbed with self-hatred because her body was satisfied while her mind told her she was doing wrong."

"No." Queenie winced.

"*I* knew her name. I knew her misery, but it was as if I was watching it or reading about it. I didn't want to see it or be near it. There was nothing I could do for her. *He's* the one with the fix-it imperative. I just wanted her misery to stop. I certainly didn't want to be a witness, but I was stuck there, week after week. If I could have shut myself off, I would."

"Mitch said he hardly ever thinks of her now."

"Why should he? To him, she's *fixed*. She's a job well done. To me, she's the memory of pain I couldn't salve."

"How do you bear it?" The question was out before she could stifle it. And this time, she couldn't excuse it by blaming Lassie Haggis.

"If it were always like that, I couldn't. Fortunately, it's not. Mostly I'm just following routines, here to there. But it's his life. His choices. It's like being given twelve books. You're obliged to read them all, but only *one* is something you're allowed to choose for yourself. The others are picked out for someone else with very different tastes. October is *my* book."

"How did you feel about me, then? When I came to The Belfry in the bus and then called the Fixer line and Mitch came to help me move my things?"

James showed his excellent teeth in a snarl. "How do you think I felt, Queenie? *I* found you. You gave *me* your wish. You felt something for me, just for a moment. Just for that moment, I thought you would come to the café with me, and we could have spent the rest of the day together . . . And maybe the night. I *longed* to have that night. And then you changed your mind, and all I could do was to let you go as gracefully as I could. I wanted you to remember me kindly, at least.

"Then, months later, he comes blundering in, trampling all over my hopes — troubling over his *blasted* she-cat — and then *you invited him into your bed.* He didn't even have to ask! He got *my* night with you as well as *my* tarts. He even got my coffee date — after a fashion, though at least you didn't take him to the O-Quay Café!"

"I did invite him to bed. And I'm not sorry. I wanted it — needed it — just like you."

"I know." He gave her a brief smile. "I'm not asking you to be sorry. You had no idea he had anything to do with me. To you, I was nothing but a man you met down at the quay one day."

Queenie thought back at some of the odd things Mitch had said to her. Had he been obliquely giving her hints that he remembered James's encounter with her? Or had it been James's memories tripping him into thinking *he* was the one who had been offered a sample tart at the quay?

James said, "After Sunday, when he comes back, will you keep on bedding him?"

"I don't know." Queenie knew there was no use prevaricating. If she was with Mitch again, James would *know.* "We didnae part well . . . and that was down to me being shrewish because I thought he was discounting me, and because — oh, because of the Curse that makes me thrawn-tongued and peevish. I don't know if he'll want anything to do wi' me again. I wouldnae blame him if he didn't. The things I said to him, and him with his hands out, pleading wi' me . . ." Tears of shame stung her eyes.

James said, unexpectedly, "If it helps, I can answer that. He *will* want you, Queenie. He'll do *anything* to be with you, just as I would. He loves you. He thinks of you all the time. And you won't *be* thrawn-tongued with him . . . right? You'll be back to the woman he helped to move to The Belfry."

"Aye. But remember, he left me to be with his cat—who doesn't even like him much. So how can he want to be with me as much as you say?"

James sat silently, with his brows drawn down. Then, he said, "There's a poem . . . something about *I couldn't love you so well if I loved not duty more.*"

"To Lucasta—Richard Lovelace," Queenie murmured.

"Yes. That's the one. The poet loves his mistress, but he loves his honour—that tells him he should go to war—more. He probably thinks that if he stayed with her, he'd be diminished in not doing his duty. Only in *his* case, it's not honour or duty he loves so much. It's not even the blasted she-cat, a thrawn creature if ever there was one. It's his love of *fixing* and making things right. I told you what happened the one time he was late taking *her* to Mum."

"You said it wasnae pretty," Queenie recalled.

James released her hands and pulled up the sleeve of his sweater, displaying a toned and muscular forearm. A long, white jagged scar ran the length of it from wrist to elbow.

"Ayesha's handiwork," he said. He pulled the sleeve down and traced his fingers up his torso from his lower ribs to his collarbone. "I have two more of them up here in parallel. It was, as you might say, a *bluidy mess.* It hurt me . . . a lot. And as for the poor beastie—she wailed and spat and hissed fit to make the bogles cringe."

Queenie stared at him, appalled. "If she's so vicious, why is she no' . . ."

"But she's not vicious! She's an ice queen. She accepts tribute with gracious purrs and winsome blinks—from him, and from Mum and Dad and the sistren . . . from Georgie and the nieves . . . from everyone *but* me. She can't bear me because I'm not him. She doesn't—can't—understand. He always takes her to Mum in the last days of September, and he stays to settle her.

"On *that* occasion, he was busy fixing something, and he left it until the thirtieth and then he overslept. He woke at eleven at night, and made a dash for it, only—he got stuck in traffic."

"But wasn't she in a cage?"

He shrugged. "Ayesha cannot be caged. She's a fay ice queen—a phaser."

Queenie didn't care to enquire further. She said, "What about your dog—your beautiful Horace? Did he hate Mitch?"

"Did Horace *bite* him, do you mean?" He gave her a faint smile. "Not a bit of it, my love. Horace was a gentleman dog. He was civil to him as he was to everyone. He'd give him a triple wag of the tail . . . and a flattening of the ears . . . but for me he'd go mad with joy. He'd *sob* when I came back. With thankfulness, I think, that we'd have more time together before he had to go where good dogs go."

His eyes, a stormy grey as he detailed Ayesha's opinion, went suddenly into the shimmering colour progression that had captivated Queenie before.

"I *loved* that dog. He was the only being in the world who loved me most and best and first and always." He put out his hands, seeking hers, and Queenie took them.

Again, she hesitated to ask what had happened to Horace. He was a short-lived breed—a brief-candle dog to go with his brief-candle master. She supposed, and hoped, he had gone where good dogs go at the ripest old age a deerhound could hope to attain. She hoped very much that James had been around to go with him as far as the living are permitted to escort those who are leaving life.

She cleared her throat—aware that James was rubbing her palms with his thumbs. "If you truly think Mitch will agree to see me—will want me still after the way I tore into him and denied him—I'll hae a straight talk with him if he'll permit it. And then, if he wants it, aye, I'll bed him."

147

He grimaced, and his thumbs stilled. "I hope he makes you happy, my love."

"Do you really? Don't answer that. I don't want to hear you lie. I'm sure you can lie very easily, even if he cannae do it. You're not a pixie."

The lift of his chin might have indicated agreement. He said, "You deserve to be loved, but I saw you first—"

Queenie interrupted, in a harder tone, "I do deserve it. But understand *this*, Master James Stuart. I dinnae need your permission to love Mitch and to be loved by him if it falls to me that way. If he forgives me for my hasty words. So—you saw me first? I dinnae care *who* saw me first. I'm no' a piece o' meat for two hoondies to snatch an' snarl over."

"No. I understand." His hands slackened around hers and he began to draw away.

"Hear me oot." Queenie tightened her grip. "I don't ask permission from you to be loved, because I want it. I deserve it. I'm no' a good person, always, but I will try to be better. I *want* a mannie in ma bed to gie me comfort an' delight."

He winced.

Queenie threw her careful decision not to lead him on to the four winds. "I *want* him. But equally, I won't ask *his* permission to love you. I will tell him as a courtesy, and because I understand that as a pixie man, he may no' be able to countenance sharing my attention with someone else. If it comes to that—if he throws it in my face or tells me to choose between ye—then I'll be done wi' the pair o' ye. I'll loe' ye both or neither—and when I'm in your arms or his, I'll spare a warm thought for the other, and hope he'll know I love him too. You may not have as much *time* to spend as he does, but you *will* have a fair and equal share of love from me."

She went on sitting there, holding hands with James Stuart, looking into his shimmering eyes and struggling to bring Mitch's features to her memory. In the back of her mind, she marvelled at the thought of complicating her already bizarre life with two fairy lovers, neither of whom was minded to share her with his other self.

"Will that work for you?" she said, when it was apparent he wasn't going to answer.

James said, quickly, eagerly, sharply, "Can I live with you, here, when it's my turn?"

"If that's what you'd like."

"I can't think of anything I'd love more . . . to wake up with you, sleep with you, hold you — cook with you, shower with you, sell tarts at the market, walk to the cove . . . take you to visit Mum and Dad, and Georgie . . ."

"That sounds like a muckle lot o' togetherness," she said, laughing. "And ye forget, I dinnae go to the markets in October."

"You *can*, with me. I'll do the selling. *You* can sit there like the queen you are. I'll even babble the Gaelic with you. I'll wear my kilt. We can be a crazy double act. I want to do everything with you. I'll store it up to think of when I can't be with you. And I'll give you an *aide memoire* to put by the bed. It will annoy *him,* but you'll never forget my face. You can kiss the picture every morning."

"I never have forgotten *your* face," she reminded him. "It's *his* I cannae remember." She added, sharply, "Is that anything to do wi' *you*, my braw laddie?"

The light died in James's eyes.

"It is, then."

"No — no! At least, not intentionally. I don't wish him any harm. I don't —"

"But you don't wish him any good, either."

"He doesn't —"

"James!" She startled them both.

He said, quietly, "To the best of my knowledge, nothing I've done has prevented you from remembering *his* face.

Unless it's because you met me first."

Queenie sighed.

He continued, "That's the truth, Queenie. And I promise, if I can be yours, I'll stop referring to Mitchell Kingsolver as *him*. I won't need to resent him because I'll have you *exclusively* for our Octobers. And—"

"Don't make too many promises, laddie. This plan depends on us *all* agreeing to share," she said soberly.

"He . . . Mitch will agree."

"But he's a pixie. I don't want him to turn green and die."

"My love, neither do I! Remember, if he goes to glory, I'm bound to go too, or vanish. But this isn't just my wishful thinking. You see, although he's a pixie, he's also a Fixer. Show him a way to make a situation right and he'll take it. He might not want to share you—he won't want that at all, any more than I do—but there's something he'll want a lot less, and that's not to have you love him.

"He'll agree. And if you have children, I can be their Auncle Jamie, who loves them and tells them subversive tales. I'll give them pups. That will annoy the blasted she-cat."

Queenie had to smile at his bubbling delight, but she cringed inwardly. What *would* people say if she had two on-again-off-again alternating lovers? However would she explain it to her children, supposing she had any?

Weel, ye daft lassie, folk talk aboot ye now, with all the lassie haggis nonsense ye've got going on.

She had another thought that made her freeze in place.

James stopped babbling and looked worried. "What is it? What did I say wrong? Was it the bit about the she-cat? I don't wish her any harm . . . and besides, she can't live forever."

"Can she no'?"

"No. She's a fay queen, but she has an allotted span."

"Weel, I'm no' feeling o'er kindly aboot that jezebel masel'. I just wondered what would happen if *we* had a child."

James looked thunderstruck. "You . . . and me?"

Queenie said, as delicately as she could, "You *can*, can't you? You're—fertile?"

"I have no idea! I've never even dared to hope—"

"How old are you, anyway?" Queenie asked.

James hesitated.

"When were you born?" she corrected.

James continued to look baffled. Finally, he said, "I wasn't born. Mitchell was born at Halloween, but these days, he celebrates his birthday in November. I—arrived—the year he was twelve, but I can't remember the date or whether I was there for the full month. Maybe Mum knows, but I think it was more gradual . . . I *do* remember one of the sistren asking Mum if *the little'un* was all right. She thought I—he—looked pale. Mum agreed he was *peely-wally*."

"You're certainly paler than Mitch," Queenie agreed. "Maybe we should give you the Halloween birthday, so you can celebrate it with me. It's mine as weel. Twenty-four, I'll be."

She closed her eyes. This was going to be *very* complicated.

James squeezed her hands to bring her attention back to him. "May I spend the night with you?"

"I told you it was just for supper."

"I know you did, but I don't want to be alone. I have so little time left to be me. You said you loved me."

"I said I *would* love you, once I've sorted things out with Mitch."

"You spent a night with h—with Mitchell—just sleeping. Can we do the same?"

"He'll know."

"Yes. But he has a lot less to *know* than I do, and *I* can handle it."

"Fine," she said, giving in abruptly. "You have first shower . . . and before you ask, I do not share showers. I never have. And get something decent to sleep in."

She flashed on Mitch's toned naked body, on his perfect olive skin.

James wouldn't be perfect. He carried three scars from the angry Ayesha.

I'll kiss them better.

She dropped her gaze to hide the desire she was sure was lighting her eyes.

James gave her hands another squeeze, raised them to his lips and kissed them with great fervency. Then he let go and got to his feet. He made his extravagant finger kissing gesture and was suddenly holding a pair of pyjamas in a startling red and green tartan.

Queenie stared him down.

"Laddie, if I'm going to li' wi' ye, and be yer October lassie until we're both auld and grey, then we're going to *have* to do something aboot your wardrobe."

Chapter Seventeen: Conversation in the Dark

Queenie Hart, October 29th, 2021

That first night with James Stuart was in no way the same as the first night Queenie spent with Mitch.

James went to the bedroom while she showered. She spent time defusing herself, clamping her mouth shut and hoping the beat of rushing water would drown any sound she made.

She hoped he had done the same.

When she finally entered the mezzanine room, he was lying in bed in his preposterous pyjamas, apparently gazing at his other self's portrait.

"James. Are you hexing my *aide-mémoire*?"

He rolled onto his back, looking up at her. His eyes were a complex tapestry of heathering. He smiled. "Queenie, would I do that? Anyway, didn't we establish that you won't hex my sporran and he won't hex your landlady?"

"You're on my side of the bed," she said. "Do you even have a sporran?"

"Wha' braeman doesnae ha' a sporran, bonnie lassie?" He chuckled at her expression. "I know this is your side, dearie. I was warming it for you."

"You were not."

"I might have been."

"Move over." She removed her gown.

James looked her over. "That's not what you usually wear

to bed."

"Noo. It's ma sark."

He sat up. "You actually have a sark."

"Aye. Once when Caledonia came calling, I bought it fro' a wee shop in the Hebrides."

"You went all the way to Scotland for a chemise?"

She shook her head. "No, laddie. I bought it online."

"Do you wear it often?"

"Never before." She shrugged. "You see, the parcel arrived in December. Until then, I hae no clue I'd made an order for replica Scottish historical clothing."

James burst into a peal of laughter. "Oh, my poor lassie!"

Queenie looked down at the garment that covered her from neck to knees. She knew objectively that it was unflattering, but tonight if felt *right*. She remembered how disgusted she'd been with herself when she opened the package she couldn't remember ordering and extracted the undyed calico garment. It bore a proud *authentically hand made in the fabled Hebrides* label, and it was shapeless.

She might have binned it, but the cost of the postage, there to see on the package, made her think twice.

She'd therefore kept it, tumbled in a bag of things she'd acquired while under the influence of the Curse. Some of them, such as the blue opaque tights she planned to wear with her Halloween costume, were beautiful or useful. Others, such as the scrap of sea glass, a tarnished apostle spoon featuring St Andrew, and a petrified oatcake, were just plain odd.

Tonight had seemed a good chance to wear the sark.

"Does it look so bad?" she ventured.

"Not at all. It becomes you at least as well as my plaid pyjamas become me." He rolled away to the other side of the bed. "Queenie, I know this must feel odd to you, but don't be scared. I won't do *anything* you don't want — don't ask for, explicitly, and even then I'll make sure you really mean it and that it's not just — what do you call it — Caledonia calling."

"If I thought ye would, ye'd no' be here."

She got in beside him.

"I'm not going to do *anything* that might make you wish you hadn't let me stay. You can put the light out. Kiss your *aide-mémoire* if you usually do."

"Aye, my bed, my rules."

He looked over his shoulder at her. "Exactly."

Queenie sat up and lifted the framed photograph from the nightstand. She stared at it, bringing Mitch's face back to her memory. She gave the picture an affectionate kiss.

May as weel start as I hope to gang on.

She kissed the picture again. *Mitch, I loe ye and I'm that sorry.*

She put it back on the nightstand.

"James . . ." She cleared her throat. "I hae a kiss for ye too, for your ainself. And after that, we sleep."

Before she could second-guess herself, she leaned down and kissed him on the mouth.

He smelled of toothpaste and wool.

She drew back. "Hae ye been using ma toothbrush, wee mannie?"

"What do *you* think?"

"I think . . . ye might easily hae conjured your ain."

"Aye, so I might," he said. And then, as she lay down again, he hitched up close and whispered in her ear, "but I didnae."

"Hmph." Queenie curled over onto her side, reached out and clicked the light.

She felt the bed give a little as James settled himself.

When she'd first slept with Mitch, she'd been so exhausted she'd barely registered his presence beyond a kiss on her cheek and a general feeling of comfort.

With James it was different. He lay quietly on his back, as far as she could judge, but she was sharply aware of him.

She waited for the change in his breathing that would

signal he was asleep, but it didn't come.

It was quiet, until she heard the flutter of the bats in the bell tower, and, faint and gentle, but undeniably *there,* the vibration of . . . something.

She felt it through her skull . . . through her teeth . . . trembling in her blood.

She sat up abruptly. "James."

"Yes?"

She'd been right. He wasn't asleep.

"What's *that*?"

He didn't say *what's what*. He listened for a few heartbeats and then she heard him exhale. "I don't know, love."

"But ye can hear it — ye ken wha' I mean?"

"I can probably hear it better than you," he said.

She remembered he'd said something similar before — or was that Mitch?

"It's no' the beasties."

"Not exactly, but I think they might be causing it," he said.

"Then what *is* it?"

"Do you remember old Master Porthwellian talking about his Kerensa's bells up in the tower? I think that's what we're hearing. The bats will be stirring, maybe getting ready for their flit back *over there* after Halloween, and they're making the bells vibrate."

Queenie shivered, hunching her shoulders. The not quite audible sounds made her feel prickly.

"*Ughhh,*" she said crossly. "I'll take ma wee besom to those hairy bahoochies if they'll no' be quiet."

"I'd love to see you with a besom," James said. He shifted beside her. "Does your Halloween costume include one?"

"It does not."

"You disappoint me. I was hoping for a full tartan explosion."

Queenie surprised herself with a giggle. As she lay down

again. "Like those pyjamas?"

"Why not?" James said. He added, "I could wear my pyjamas to the ball."

Queenie drew breath to snap that he most definitely could *not*, but just in time she recalled her promise to be a nicer person.

"I told ye to wear what ye please to the ball," she said.

"But that was when you said you wouldn't trade for kisses. Now you've given me one, I feel bound to please you by looking my best in my kilt."

Queenie bolted upright again. "That was nae trade! It was — was —"

"I know what it was," he said. "But I will wear my kilt. It's time."

Queenie rubbed her temples. The phantom sound of the bells made her prickle all over.

She remembered her second night with Mitch, when her body had taken over and she'd scrambled on top of him. He'd helped her, accommodated her, and it had been wonderful.

She breathed in hard, trying to dispel the desire to have James right here and right now.

The scent of clean wool came to her again, mixed slightly with her toothpaste.

"You don't smell like Mitch," she said abruptly.

"So I've been told."

"By whom?" She felt a jolt of jealousy at the idea someone else might have been close to both her men.

It was odd that she could accept that each of them had had lovers, even though James's could be only short term, but the idea that they had both had the same woman made her cross.

He laughed. "Mum, of course. Being a braeside lassie, Mum has met a mani-man or three — her grandad had a howling blue savage mani with a high devotion to woad. Mum can just remember the Pict . . . she says her granny used to say *Come awa' lassie, the Pict is aboot today and ye dinnae need to see his willie coloured that way . . .* With the Pict in her memory, she was nervous when I emerged. She's glad I'm not a howling blue savage, but she did let fall she finds my *bouquet des fees* a wee bit unnerving. The Pict smelled like wet fleece, heavy on the lanoline, you see."

"You smell good," she said.

"I'm glad you think so."

She rubbed her ears and her neck again, her teeth tingling. "James. Can you make it *stop*?"

"I can't keep the beasties from shuttling about, but I can cast a glamour, if you like."

"Please do."

She felt a slight jerk in the bed, and the maddening sensation snapped off like a light going out.

Queenie lay down again and relaxed. "Do you always kiss your fingers when you conjure or cast a glamour?"

"Not always."

"Why?"

"If you recall, I conjured a chair to the kitchen for you when you had your tumble. My hands were engaged with supporting my glorious armful of lassie."

"Then why do it at all if you don't have to?"

He seemed stumped by the question.

Queenie hitched up on her elbow, facing him in the dark, waiting expectantly.

"I have no idea," he said at last. "Better ask h—Mitch the same question and see if he can tell you."

"He doesn't do it, though. He double taps his wrist."

James laughed. "Not always, my love."

"No—no, you're right. I'm sure he conjures things when he's driving Ethel, but of course he doesn't let go of the wheel to do it. How odd."

"I suppose it is."

"And you really don't know."

"I really don't know. I suspect we do it . . . when we do it . . . as a kind of courtesy so others *know* we're about to do it."

"I see. When you and Mitch swap places, do you do anything special?"

"I can't speak for Mitch, but when my time in the ascendent is over I know *I* don't do anything. Quite the opposite. I picture myself being dragged towards the edge of a cliff and I hold on to my time for dear life."

"I'm sorry."

"Don't be. This time it will be better. I can't say I'll go willingly, but I promise I won't resist him this time, and I won't resent him. You see, I know the sooner you get things sorted out with *him*, the sooner I can start dreaming of next time." He was quiet for a few seconds and then he said, "Will you really spare me a loving thought when you're with Mitch?"

"I promise. I'll kiss him twice, and one of those will be for you. Will you know?"

"Yes, if you think of me. He'll know too, I expect."

"Good."

"I love being here with you so much, you can't imagine," he said into the dark.

Queenie couldn't reply.

"You see, this is *mine*. All for me. Mitch has never had this."

"But ye *know* he has," she said.

"Not this. No. He's had Queenie, the Queen of Tarts, but he's never slept with the October lassie in his arms . . . and he never will."

"Neither have you, yet, but you will."

"Next year."

"Now." Queenie squirmed closer, located him with her fingertips and put her head on his shoulder. His arm came around her.

She said, "I know I said we should just sleep, but I'm not

sleepy. Will you tell me about the wish I made?"

"You know about it already. You wished me sweet dreams, luck, and love."

"Och, I ken fine what I said, sheepheid, I mean aboot the wee scrap o' tartan."

James tightened his arm. "There's not much to tell, but here goes . . . I told you Georgiana made me the hugging toy when she made some for her own bairns. She gave me Horace, and she cared for him when I was away. But that's not the only thing she did for me." He paused. "You might not like to hear this."

"Go on."

"If you remember, I told you Mum's dad, Granddad Donald Stuart, gave me a kilt when Mitch got enough years. Actually, he gave it to me the day before Mitch's birthday, because *he* celebrates on November the first, for obvious reasons. I received my kilt on Mitch's real birthday, with all Granddad's spiel on what it means when a braeman gets his kilt."

"Don't wee laddies wear them?"

"Sometimes, *over there,* but this kilt is *the* kilt. The kilt of the *man grown.* It signifies all sorts of things. I was happy and proud to have it, but I knew I'd be gone the next day, and I wouldn't be able to take full advantage of all its significance. Still, I put it on and wore it, and Granddad approved. Granny Elspeth said I looked *verra fine,* and then she went into the bothy and brought me some shortbread. I showed the sistren and my parents, of course, and then I went to show it to Georgiana."

"Did she like it?"

"She—broke down and cried," James said.

"Why? Was she in love with you?" It seemed likely.

"Nothing like that, love. It wouldn't be seemly, and besides, she was nearly thirty, and heavy with her third bairn.

He – Mitch, I mean – would have discovered the trouble in a minute or so and fixed it, but then he wouldn't have made her cry in the first place. Because it was me, she just kept on weeping, and hugging me.

"Finally, her man came and peeled her off me, and got her into their house to lie down."

"Did you ever find out what was wrong?" Queenie asked.

"I did. Her man came out to see me after a bit. He was good about it. He's a good sort of person – but he's a pixie man, and of course his focus was on his lassie and their bairns. Still, he spared the time to explain to me that Georgie was all right and would see me again next time . . ."

"That sounds a poor explanation to me," Queenie said. She felt James shift, as if the memory disturbed him, and she brought her free arm across his chest.

"When I asked if I'd upset her somehow, he said, no, it was just that having me wear a man's kilt made her see me as *man grown* as we say *over there*. And she saw I could never have what she has with her man."

"What did you do?" Queenie asked.

"I thanked him, and took myself off, and I packed the kilt away in lavender. I never put it on again."

Queenie bit her lip. "Ye dinnae have to wear it to the ball."

"I *want* to. I want to please you."

Queenie realised she was stroking his neck and shoulder inside the pyjamas. She knew she should stop, but it felt natural and good. "Do ye mind?" She tapped her fingers in explanation.

"What do you think?"

"That's all right, then." She wanted to roll in more and start kissing his chest, but that would be going too far. To distract herself, she said, "You still havenae told me about the wee scrap of tartan."

"So I haven't." He moved a little, so his cheek was against

her hair. "The next time it was my turn, I went to see Georgie, and to meet my new nievie, who was toddling about by then. I'd watched her growing, because Mitch had, but of course she had no idea who the strange man was. Georgie was a bit embarrassed. She said not to mind her, because carrying made her emotional. When my last day came around, her man came to find me. He said she'd made me a gift, but she didn't want to make an eedjit of herself a second time, so she'd asked him to bring it."

"It was the wish," Queenie guessed.

"Indeed. She made it from a piece of cloth she had left over from making the hugging toys. Her man said it was mine to do whatever I wanted with — to use it for myself, or to give it away."

"And you gave it to *me*," Queenie said.

"I did. I couldn't think what to wish for — because wishes have to be *possible*, and within the gift of the person who facilitates them. I couldn't have wished to be a full-time man, or to take over as the main man, or — well, I couldn't think of *anything* that would work. I couldn't wish my dear Horace back, or for it to be always October. Neither could I wish for material things, except in the peripheral sense . . . and besides, what do *I* need?

"Having the thing in my pocket started to scratch at my mind. Georgie meant it as a kind act — she's the kindest person I know — save one. Oddly, she'd a wee bit like Mitch. She's not a Fixer, or even a pixie, but she's motherly. She wants people she loves to be happy. I couldn't bring myself to use her gift for just anything, and it seemed churlish to waste it, as I did the hugging toy, so I put it in the lap of fate. I took it down to Circular Quay and I decided I'd give it to the first person I met who needed it."

"Me," Queenie murmured.

"Yes — you intrigued me. You were so splendid and so

scared—and you gave me what you had without counting it or checking you weren't accidentally giving me a fistful of two-dollar coins. You accepted the wish, and I hoped you'd wish something splendid to make your life better. And then you turned around and you spent it on *me*. And you gave me your card—And then I came to you and *almost*—" He broke off.

"Aye, almost," she agreed.

"And then, of all the moving firms and all the handymen in the country, you chose to call Mitch."

"Aye, but I called a muckle many before him. He was the only one who would help."

James sighed. "That's the last of it. The whole story from my perspective. You'll have to get the rest of it from Mitch."

"Aye. James, would it help if you wrote him a letter?"

"I doubt it. There's no point really, since he'll know it already."

"He'll know I'm sorry for being horrible to him?"

"He'll know. But love, you were horrible, as you put it, because of the way he behaved. He got himself into a corner."

She nodded against his chest and absently rubbed her cheek against the soft cloth of his pyjamas. They were startlingly ugly, but they felt nice in the dark.

"He probably won't be able to stop behaving like that," James said. "I don't have the imperative myself, but I can tell when it's upon him."

"He'll have to do what he has to do, and I'll have to accept it." Queenie was at last feeling sleepy, but something stirred in her mind, preventing it from closing down. At first, she suspected the glamour James had cast on the bells in the belltower was degrading, but after a while, she recognised it as an idea.

"James."

"Hmm?" He gave her a squeeze.

163

"I had a thought. What if Mitch has been trying to fix us—you and me?" It seemed a preposterous notion, but the more she thought it through, the more traction it gained in her mind.

"He's been so helpful, and he gave me some little almost-hints. What if what he wanted to tell me so badly was that I should open my heart to you as well?"

"That's a beautiful idea, my love, and I wish I could believe it, but I *know* him, and I doubt if it's so."

Chapter Eighteen: A Kiss for Mitch

Queenie Hart, October 30th, 2021

James stayed for breakfast. Queenie would willingly have spent the whole day with him, but he explained he had to be off to visit his family and to take his leave of them. "I don't leave it until Halloween these days—I learned not to leave things until the last minute when the she-devil exploded at me."

"Will you tell them about me?"

"They know about you already."

"What—how?"

"Mitch told Mum when he fetched your currants—"

"Oh, o' course he did."

"And more when he took the she-devil for her visit."

"What, exactly?"

"I don't know. I tend to tune out as much as possible when Mitch goes to see Mum. She loves me dearly, but he was her only son for years."

"Will you tell her anything about me?"

"I will—and I'll tell her I have a chance to be happier than I ever dreamed, but I can't tell her any details of our future because it's really up to *him* to sort out our dynamics. I don't have the time, and he's the one with the biggest adjustment to make. "

"How?" she asked.

"I've managed to use his name last night and this morning, right?"

"Aye."

"It wasn't even difficult once I got over the resentment. But for Mitch it's not a matter of using my name. He has to learn to talk about me at all, and to admit to himself, and to you, that I'm me, and not an aberration. I doubt if you're prepared to spend most of a year avoiding my name."

"I am no," she said decidedly.

"I'm glad, because you promised to think of me and love me, *often,* and you can't do that if Mitch won't allow you to mention me, or to kiss him while thinking of me."

"Allowing willnae come into it."

"Of course not," he said quickly. "There will be no allowing, no claiming and no—what was the word you used? Was it *managing*?"

"It was. And it works three ways. I'll not accept *claiming* or managing or allowing from either of you. I told you—I'll hae the pair o' ye or neither. But I'll also no' try to do it to you. You'll be coming to live with me on the first of October next year . . . always supposing I get to extend my lease. I dinnae know what Oliver will do."

James nodded. "Expect me at a moment after midnight, my love. As for Oliver, the old fiend, he likes you and he wants you to be happy. I should think having you in his Belfry and your tarts and shortbread in his belly will extend his already impressive span quite considerably."

Queenie smiled, thinking of her eldest landlord. "I hope so, the auld diel." She was about to say it would be fun to meet him in the flesh when he came to unward the door when she recalled that James would be gone by then. Maybe Mitch would be there.

"But Mitch—will he want to live with me too?"

"I expect so, but there might be a wee impediment to that."

Queenie inspected his charming and increasingly beloved face for smugness, and she found none.

"If you're talking about Ayesha, it might not be so wee," she said.

James pushed away his porridge bowl.

Queenie got up from her seat and edged around the table. "Hoosh back, wee mannie," she said.

James pushed his chair away from the table, and she slid into his lap, winding an arm around his neck.

"I'm wishfu' for a wee bitty snuggle," she announced.

James kissed her cheek, working his way around to her lips.

Queenie felt like purring.

Unfortunately, that reminded her of the impediment.

"Yon moggy hates to be disrupted," she said, when she could free her mouth.

James said, "She does," separating the words with a kiss.

"If Mitch comes to live here, even part of the time, does that mean I have to have his ice queen too?"

"I think that will be up to you. Your Belfry. Your rules."

"But what do you—"

James stopped her by kissing her again. When he finished, he said, "If you want to hold to sorting things with Mitch before you take another lover, you'd best get off my lap, dearie. Explosions are imminent."

Queenie drew back and brought his face into focus. His eyes were cycling through their colours. "That's so bonnie," she said breathlessly. She ducked her head to kiss his cheek and got up reluctantly. "I'm gey sorry to make ye hot and hard, Jamie."

James smiled at her. "That's a fib, Queenie Hart."

"Just a wee one. But what aboot yon moggy?"

"Yon moggy detests me, so you'll have to sort that aspect out with Mitch. And if he and she do move in here with you, then you'll have to see to it that he *never* leaves it too late to relocate her in September. I have no fancy to wake on my first joyful morning with you and get shredded for my pains. She rouses Mitch by patting his cheek with her paw. I don't want a face full of claws when she discovers she's waking the wrong man."

Queenie stood back, wincing at the thought. "I'll be awa' to my baking, an' ye gang to see your mum and da—will ye be coming back here tonight?"

"Yes. Supper and then bed. Your bed. Your rules."

"Guid." Queenie went the cupboard and fetched the container in which Mitch had brought her currants. She loaded in some shortbread and tartan tarts. "Gi' these to her wi' my thanks."

James took the container. He held it for a moment and then it vanished.

"Ye no' kissed your fingers."

"No. I have a lassie to kiss."

Queenie went into his arms, almost without reservation. She kissed him, revelling in his warmth, his scent and the strength of his arms.

"It's no' like kissing Mitch," she said when she came up for air.

"Good," James said.

He didn't ask for details, and Queenie was glad, because she couldn't explain it, even to herself.

Instead, he said, "If you want to give me a kiss for him, I won't mind. And before you start wondering if I'm being devious, I won't try to withhold it, or to hijack it, or to divert it, or to use it to gain information or to prove a point."

Still in his arms, Queenie squinted at him with suspicion. "How long hae ye been preparing *that* wee speech, laddie?"

"Ever since last night," he said.

"Then ye've thought it through."

He freed one hand and kissed his fingers, caught a picture frame out of the air and presented it to Queenie. "You'll need your *aide-mémoire.*"

Queenie noted that James was encroaching again. He'd conjured something of hers without asking permission . . . and it had worked. Ergo, he had the right to do it.

She patted his cheek before remembering that was what Ayesha did.

There'll be a reckoning betwixt ye and me, my fine thrawn moggy.

"I wish I could have known Horace," she said.

"He'd have loved you."

Queenie took the frame from James, and she gazed at the photograph. Mitchell Kingsolver smiled back at her. It was a posed photo, maybe a selfie. She realised she hadn't asked its provenance. She preferred the one she had snapped on her phone, catching him unawares. She wished she could picture it in her mind, and she *really* wished she hadn't deleted it.

Maybe some technological whiz could somehow restore it?

Certainly not Mitch . . . he's a real klutz with technology.

She remembered James chopping vegetables lightning fast with a lethal-looking knife.

"James, I deleted my photo of Mitch from my phone. Is there any chance you could get it back for me?"

He shook his head. "Sorry, love. But on the bright side, you can snap another one next week."

"I'll have one of you, anyway." She fished out her phone and aimed it at him. Then she changed her mind. "I want one of the two of us together."

"Tomorrow night," he said.

"Aye, at the ball. Noo for that kiss."

She held the *aide-mémoire* before her, but that was going to be impossible. In the end, she laid it aside and flung herself at James, channelling the way she'd once greeted Mitch.

Love, that was the best greeting I've ever had.

His words, spoken in his warm voice, echoed through her mind, and for a moment it *was* Mitch, kissing her back, arms hard around her, subtly different from the way James held her.

O' course! He has his left hand high and his right hand . . . She giggled, feeling a warm hand cupping her bottom in a possessive caress.

She flexed her muscles and then broke the kiss and stepped back. "That was for Mitch."

James nodded, his eyes flaring with colour.

"And this one, my darling laddie, is for you."

She closed in more slowly, feeling his hands loosely clasped around her back, and she kissed him with affection and promise.

"Noo, off wi' ye, laddie," she said, and James left.

The day passed quite quickly. From time to time, Queenie was aware of the bats in the belltower, and of the subliminal sound of the bells' vibration. She tried to ignore it, but she was relieved when she heard Ethel on the gravel.

She ran to the door, but before she reached it, it burst open, and James stepped inside. He had his arms out, and she fell into them.

Something was different. He seemed tense.

Queenie kissed his throat. "What is it?" she asked.

"Nothing wrong."

"What, though?"

He said, rapidly, "I talked to Mum about you. I showed her your picture."

Queenie frowned. "But we haven't taken one yet."

"I made a print of the one on Mitch's phone," he said.

"Och, I'd no' thought o' that." In fact, she'd forgotten about it entirely.

"It's not a very good one, but Mum was pleased to see what you look like. She thinks you're bonnie, by the way. She sent something for you . . . but only if you would truly like it. She won't mind if you'd rather not. I won't mind."

"Jamie, whatever are ye babbling aboot?"

James fished in his pocket and lifted out a gold chain. He handed it to Queenie.

She took it mechanically. It was made of soft red gold that gleamed with a magical glow. From it hung a pendant made in the form of a Scottish thistle, carved out of purple stone.

"That's a heather gem, from Heather Isle in the Star Pin," James said. "The Pict gave it to my great-granny . . ."

"It's *beautiful*," Queenie said, "But Jamie, I cannae possibly take something so precious. Your mum—"

"Mum wants you to have it. She can't give it the sistren, because there are three of them—besides, they have wedding necklaces from their men. Would you at least wear it to the ball for me?"

Queenie held it up. It was beautiful, striking and thoroughly OTT. It would look perfect with her costume, as Jacaranda Fairling had described it.

She handed it back to James and then turned away, lifting her hair clear of her collar. "Put it on for me, Jamie," she said.

He did up the catch and then she turned to face him, raising her face for a kiss.

Then she dropped her face into his shoulder.

"Queenie, do you want to give one for Mitch now?" he asked.

She shook her head. "No' now. This is *our* wee time, yours and mine."

Chapter Nineteen: Watershed

Queenie Hart, October 31st, 2021

Halloween dawned with a fearsome flutter and scutter and a humming of bells in the belltower.

Queenie raised her head from James's shoulder and grumbled a protest.

James kissed his fingers, and the noise stopped.

Staying in bed was out of the question, but neither did Queenie want to be on her own in her solitary routine.

She kissed her *aide-mémoire* and then James, as Mitch's proxy, and then she kissed James for his ain self. Then they got up. James vanished into the bathroom while Queenie began on breakfast, and then she took her turn while he made the tea.

"What shall we do today?" he asked eagerly.

Queenie said, "Wha' I'd love to do is to go to the city and hae that date at the O-Quay Café."

"*Really?*" His eyes turned lavender.

"Really, ye daft laddie." Queenie laughed. "If I seem aboot to call some auld haggis a daft she-baw, ye'll need to pu' a stop to it, aye?"

"Like this." He pulled her close and kissed her.

"Aye, and if yon eyes start wi' the heathering, I'll hide them like *this*." She dragged his head down.

James hugged her. "And you'll wear what you had on the day we met?"

"Aye, flour an' all." She ostentatiously ran her hand over

her breasts. "Nae need to wonder wha' ye'll be wearing, laddie."

James blinked and swallowed audibly. Then he glanced down at himself. "You said something about my wardrobe."

"Aye! Maybe we could buy ye a new sweater at least!"

Then she remembered something. "What aboot the bus?"

James said, "I'll do the first run and then ask Olivier if he'll do the midday one. I'll tell him I have a date. He can take Nessa with him . . . his girl."

With that settled, Queenie went to look out the clothing she had worn the year before.

It wasn't her smartest outfit, because she'd been dressed for a day of writing her blog and sorting recipes when she fled the unit, but it would do.

James drove her, and some other passengers, to Borrowdale Junction, where he handed over Ethel and the keys to Olivier and his silver-clinking girlfriend.

They sat side by side in the train, and James had his arm around her, now and then kissing her hair.

At Circular Quay, they walked around, people-watching and enjoying the spring. They went up through the Rocks and shopped for a sweater for James.

Queenie was tempted to take him to Fairings, but she had no idea if the ladies there made sweaters, and she wanted him to have one now — today — for his birthday.

He had no idea of his size, and Queenie had to guess. She saw him eyeing a bright red one which would have clashed with his hair, but he finally selected one in navy.

"Verra handsome," Queenie opined, when he came out of the changing room.

Queenie paid for it, because, as she said, it was at her insistence that he'd bought it, and, with his argyle sweater in her bag, they headed for the O-Quay Café.

Queenie blushed as they entered, for fear of being

disapproved of by the staff, but the waitress served her with no sign of recognition. She blew out her cheeks with relief.

James crossed his eyes at her. "Shall we order tarts?"

"We'll no' do that, daft laddie."

"Liquorice bats, then," he said gleefully, finding that dainty on the specials board.

He ordered some and they were just as revolting as Queenie expected.

After that, they caught a ferry and rode to Cremorne to enjoy the point walk and then wandered the fairy gardens at Windhill before returning to The Belfry at six for a quick dinner.

"You said you'd pick me up at seven-thirty," Queenie said, remembering.

"So I did." James poured the tea. "I'll go away for half an hour and then come back for you."

"Noo, ye daftie! Unless ye need to?"

"I do—I'm picking up one or two passengers for the ball . . . but not just yet."

She rubbed her face. "I'm all salty fro' the ferry ride."

"Better have a shower," he said.

She got up from the table. "Aye . . . I'd no' be draggle-tailed an' briny at the ball." She headed for the bathroom. Some imp made her add, over her shoulder, "Come in a wee while an' wash my back."

His remarkable eyes glowed in a tapestry of heather colouring.

A second imp told Queenie this was a bad idea, and not fair to him, or to Mitch.

She growled at it.

She had never shared a shower with a friend or lover. She was going to break the habit of a lifetime for James. Mitch would just have to understand.

He can have his shower wi' me tomorrow.

She was under the spray, with her hair tied up in a

towelling cap, when James came in. He was wearing—his startling plaid pyjamas.

Queenie looked at him severely.

He glanced down at her body, streaming with water and wreathed in vapour, and then he lifted his gaze back to her face.

"Ye're *no'* going to shower in those," she said.

James shrugged. "Your shower. Your rules." He kissed his fingers, still gazing at her face.

The pyjamas vanished.

Queenie repaid him the compliment of a brief once-over.

Mitch had perfect skin, smooth and glowing.

James was pale, neatly made, marred with three vicious scars from his encounter with Ayesha.

She was glad to see they'd healed without puckering.

She didn't mention them. Neither did he. Everyone had scars. James's showed to the naked eye. So what?

They regarded one another through the sheeting water, and then Queenie hauled him into the shower and presented him with the soap and her back.

She felt his hands smoothing over her shoulders. She smelled something unexpected and delicious.

"Jamie, wha's that?"

"Mum's honey and milk soap, dearie. I'll leave it with you. Mitch prefers the one she makes with nut butter."

Ouch. Even in the matter o' soap he has to defer to someone else's taste for eleven months o' the year.

"Thank ye, Jamie. It's delightful."

"What would you like for your birthday?" he asked.

She slithered around into his arms. "The thistle necklace is what I like . . . I cannae say I'll wear it every day, but wear it I will, when I hae the occasion."

"*I* have the occasion to wear my kilt," he said. He stepped back, soaped himself quickly, handed her the tablet of soap, rinsed, and stepped out of the shower.

With a kiss of his fingers, he was wrapped in a gaudy beach towel printed with palm trees.

Queenie laughed.

James said, "I'll get dressed, and then go and fetch Kez and the others. I'll meet you back here at seven-thirty."

He was out the door before she could respond.

Queenie went on standing under the water.

Watershed moment.

Her eyes prickled and she splashed her face, blinking furiously.

Tomorrow she might be showering with Mitch, negotiating terms, making promises she would keep.

Or else it might all be over.

She stepped out of the shower, dried off and headed to the mezzanine bedroom.

The bats fluttered. The bells silently boomed. Queenie marched down to the narthex, clad in her milk and honey skin.

She gasped.

Leaning against the warded door was a besom.

Chapter Twenty: The Halloween Ball

Queenie Hart, October 31st — November 1st, 2021

Queenie hitched herself into her Halloween costume, one boob at a time, and glanced down at her impressive cleavage.

She assessed her reflection in the tall looking glass with her gaze shifting from her Victorian button boots up her long legs in the blue tights to the top of her puffed up hair.

"No' a tartan in sight. Ye'll do, lassie," she remarked.

Faint heart never won fair laddie . . .

The laddie was hers for the asking. It was the pixie man that might cause her some problems.

Both or neither. Neither or both.

She touched the extravagantly lovely thistle pendant that dangled *just so* from its red gold chain.

Should I hae accepted this? Och, but how could I hae disappointed him, again?

And disappointed ye'sel' . . .

She laughed. The Queen of Tarts looked back at her, clothed in brocade and silk and fantastical embroidery, and she was magnificent.

It was half past seven. She swept down the shallow steps, traversed the main room, and stopped by the warded door.

A quick snatch and she had the besom in her hand. She raised it menacingly and brandished it.

"Aye, flutter weel, ma fine wee batty friends . . . tomorrow

I'll hae ye oot o' there, begad!" She beat a swift tattoo on the door with the besom.

Silence fell.

Queenie put down the besom.

"Until next year, then, my dearies," she said cordially. She swung on the full-length purple cape that had come with the costume, picked up the box of Cathedral Window tarts she was taking to the ball, and swaggered out of The Belfry to meet the bus.

James had more than a couple of passengers.

Kez, dressed in an evening dress straight from the nineteen fifties, grinned at her and waved her hand grandly.

"Hi, love. The Chess-Nuts and I decided to make a night of it. Not often we get driven anywhere by a man in a kilt. We've taken the vote. James must *always* wear his kilt *and* tell us what he wears underneath." She cackled.

"Not blooming likely," James said. He smiled at Queenie. "Sit by me, my darling love."

Kez hooted and then fanned herself with a paper plate. The Chess-Nuts, whom Queenie belatedly recognised as the group of friends who played chess together on the village green, thumped their walking sticks in gleeful chorus.

"Ye've created a monster, Jamie," Queenie said.

He shrugged. "Let it go."

Ethel pulled away from The Belfry, and Queenie said, "Thanks for the besom, laddie."

"You're welcome. Have you brought it with you?"

"Noo—"

James kissed his fingers.

The besom landed against Queenie's knees.

"Now you have."

Queenie reflected that this was going to be the most surreal night ever.

She wasn't wrong.

They arrived at Oakengrove, and James lifted Queenie down, besom and all, kissing her as he did so.

He helped the Chess-Nuts down after that, kissing each one's hand as she alighted.

Queenie held back a mix of laughter and tears. He wasn't her Fixer, and he had no imperative to *fix* things, but he was doing his part in giving the Chess-Nuts a night out to remember.

Oakengrove was floodlit, so Queenie got to appreciate James's costume to the full.

He'd gone the whole way, in blue-grey Stuart tartan. Although Queenie was somewhat of an expert on kilts, she couldn't recognise this one. It wasn't the great kilt type with metres of bunched fabric, but neither was it the modern *féileadh beag*, or little wrap. It might be a walking kilt, or an eight-yard kilt.

She gave up trying to identify it and just revelled in watching a man, *her* man, moving with easy confidence in a garment he was born to wear. The full pleats rippled and swung, and he'd chosen to wear it with his new sweater, dark kilt hose and contrasting flashes.

Once he had the Chess-Nuts disembarked, he stood back to let them enter the big house first.

Then he offered his arm to Queenie. "My love."

"Ma laddie." She removed her cloak. "James, would ye put this back in Ethel?"

He made no move.

Queenie tossed the cloak to him. It fell at his feet, lay there for a moment, then vanished.

James stared at her.

Queenie grasped the besom, holding it like a sceptre. She felt *right*. "Weel, laddie?"

"Queenie Hart, Queen of *my* heart, you are glorious."

She swept him a curtsey. "So are ye, my laddie. The mun

o' my dreams."

He offered his arm again, and they went into the ball.

James could dance.

Queenie wondered how she could ever have doubted it.

She had a chance to appreciate him in full as he took Kez for a slow turn, making her laugh. He danced with such of the Chess-Nuts who were up for it, then with Willow Dee, and Maureen Tucker.

Queenie, meanwhile, danced with Duncan and Bernie, each of whom eyed her with bemusement and asked her if she was feeling better.

"Aye, grand," she said, allowing her *r* to roll as it would.

She was back with James when a party of six people arrived, all wearing black cloaks. At least, they were as they stepped into the ballroom.

A second later, the cloaks had vanished.

The three men wore leggings with embroidered tabards, giving them the look of mediaeval heralds, and the women were in floor-length shifts covered with overlays of floating colour with braided girdles and wreaths of silk flowers.

The youngest man saw Queenie and hurried over, towing a dark-haired young woman who looked a few years older. His marigold leggings matched the base colour of her shift.

He came to a stop. "All hail to the Queen of Tarts!" he exclaimed, executing a deep bow.

Queenie grinned at him, recognising his delicate features and shy smile as he came upright before her. "Asher . . . are ye here for tarts?"

He said, "Have you brought any?"

"Well noo . . ." Queenie glanced at James. "Jamie, this is Asher, who helped me find Fairings when I went to order my wee costume. And I expect ye'll be Jessie, the laddie's lover," she said to the young woman.

Jessie raised one eyebrow with a quick smile. "I expect I

am," she said. She looked at Queenie with frank assessment. "Mind, sweet, I wouldn't turn *you* down, if you were on offer."

Asher said, seriously, "I'm Jessie's forever man . . . but she's still on the lookout for a forever maid."

"Weel, she'll no' be havin' me," Queenie said.

"You don't feel able to share?" Jessie asked.

"I wouldnae say that . . . This is my Jamie."

Jessie said, "Very nice, too. I assume your Jamie is the source of that glorious heather gem necklace?"

"Aye." Queenie looked down to where the carved thistle spat light from its facets.

Jessie touched her wrist, drawing attention to a gold bracelet hung with a sparkling yellow heart. "I'll raise you a sungelt stone . . . from my Asher. He claims me as his life's sunrise, which is a poetic way of reminding me I taught him his horizontal manners."

Honour satisfied, Queenie examined the bracelet. It was charming, and she said so without reserve.

She'd read quite a bit about fay jewellery in her books. The piskies she knew all wore silver, but she'd seen some gold and copper pieces illustrated in *The Fay Companion*. She was sure her gold and purple thistle outshone every piece she'd seen, and she wondered at the love and generosity that had caused James's mother Danna to gift it to a stranger.

But Mitch said a gift to me was a gift to him . . .

This is her way of assuring them that they both are her blood and her beloved sons.

Currants were a long way from statement jewellery, but she supposed the theory was the same. Danna loved her boys.

By then, the other two couples had approached. Queenie recognised the women without surprise as Jacaranda Fairling and her partner, Lucida, along with men who were presumably their husbands. Asher was clearly Lucida's son, for he looked very like her husband. He obviously had hidden depths, if the capricious Jessie had chosen him for more than a passing fling.

She locked eyes with Jacaranda. "Ye didnae say ye'd be here tonicht."

"Well, Your Majesty, how could we not come? We wanted to see you and—" She glanced at James.

"This is Jamie," Queenie said. "Jamie, these are the ladies who made ma costume."

Jacaranda smiled in greeting, then her gaze sharpened on James. "You're James Stuart . . . right?"

"Aye," he said.

"Son of my old friend Danna Stuart—Danna Kingsolver, if I'm not mistaken?"

"I am."

Jacaranda relaxed, as if something had been explained. "Well, my dear, next time you see Danna, tell her I still have her recipe for marigold sovereign, and I find it invaluable. And now I see you're the perfect match for Queenie. The day I met her I thought she might be twins, you see."

"Only child," Queenie reminded her.

"Not quite, my dear—but I'm glad you came to us." With another quick smile, she took her husband's hand and drew him into the dance.

Jessie and Asher went too, leaving Lucida standing with her quiet elf man.

Queenie felt tears gathering. *My perfect laddie.*

Lucida looked at her with her startled doe's eyes. "Dear one, it may be all right."

"How?"

The woman stepped forward enveloping Queenie in a cloud of soft perfume like pansies in the morning. She got up on tiptoe to whisper in Queenie's ear, and the sounds of the ball suddenly vanished.

"I'll tell you what to do—but you should do it *only* if your heart is moved to follow my words. Do you understand?" She stood back, and there was a sparkle of apprehension in her eyes. She took Queenie's hands. "*Only* if your heart is moved to open your eyes to truth. Because if not . . . you can still lose."

"Tell me." Queenie's voice shook in her own ears.

Lucida let go of her hands, reached out and traced the three linked hearts embroidered on the neckline of Queenie's bodice.

"Link the hearts," she said.

She stepped back, raising one hand.

The sounds of the ball returned.

James handed Queenie her besom. "What was that all about?" he asked.

Queenie said, "I'm not too sure, Jamie. Can ye conjure that spare box o' tarts fro' the fridge at home for wee Asher?"

James kissed his fingers. "Done. When do you want the tarts from Ethel?"

"Och, noo . . . they're serving supper."

A huge cauldron of pumpkin soup had arrived, and the Oakengrove kitchen staff were serving it into wide-mouthed mugs, along with rolls from Our Daily Bread, the local bakery.

Grated cheese, parsley, sour cream and other accompaniments flanked the cauldron, and the contributions from the guests lined up on another long table.

When James conjured them in, Queenie carried her tarts to add to the selection.

She produced her phone from a deep pocket in her costume, but James, seeing it, shook his head.

"Maureen and Nona are taking photos of folk in their costumes for the *Strad*," he said.

"An' ye think they might take one for us?"

"I'm sure they would." He tugged her to the small queue

that had lined up on the stage at the back of the ballroom.

There was a choice of three sets of seats with backdrops. When it was their turn, James and Queenie chose plain wooden chairs against a black background.

Maureen took their photos, and she agreed to send copies to Queenie. She raised her brows at James. "Do you want copies, too, James?"

"I'll share Queenie's," he said.

Maureen nodded as if that was perfectly reasonable.

Supper lasted for an hour, then dancing resumed.

At eleven o'clock, the lights dimmed, and a spinning projector set shadows of bats, witches on brooms, and other motifs flitting about the walls.

Coloured lights followed, until Queenie felt she was dancing in a giant ball of stained glass.

She swayed dreamily with her head against James's shoulder. It should have been perfect, and it almost was.

His time was running out.

She wished suddenly that they had gone back to The Belfry after supper.

She could have taken James to bed and held him there.

Too late now, lassie.

Cutting it fine.

Link the hearts.

She remembered a Halloween ballad — Tam Lin — in which a man was beguiled by the fairy queen. His human lover won the right to take him home *if* she could hold onto him.

She'd held her man, while he'd turned into all manner of frightening and painful things, but she'd triumphed.

If only I could hold my Jamie.

That was ridiculous. No fairy queen had James in thrall. Holding him, keeping him, would take away Mitch's agency.

Love both or neither, lassie. Dinnae regret the one when the other is nigh. That's the way it maun go.

She began to feel nervous as well as sad.

What would happen when James slipped away . . . when Mitch returned? Would he be angry with her? Naked? Mortified? Bewildered to find himself at a Halloween Ball?

She held James closer.

Time poured through their hourglass.

The lights went out.

The music ceased.

A clock began to strike midnight.

A woman's voice, a powerful alto, sang acapella into the dark.

"From ghoulies and ghosties

long-leggedy beasties

and things that go bump in the night,

Good Lord deliver us.

Good Lord deliver us.

Good Lord deliver us."

Queenie's back prickled.

Her time had run out.

Just before the clock finished striking, she knew what she had to do.

She reached up on tiptoe, and she whispered, "Jamie, my ain, I'll love ye forever, and I'll see ye in a wee while." She kissed him with all the promise she could muster.

She *felt* the change.

The lips on hers were subtly different, and the hands that held her close had changed their orientation.

"Darling laddie," she tried to say, but her head spun, and the soft, fresh scent of eucalyptus drifted up from the warm throat so close to her.

She went on kissing Mitch until she felt his lips part in a gasp. He swayed.

Shock.

The lights came up, soft like lanterns, and dancers blinked and shuffled, possibly disoriented by the show of light and sound and silence, and possibly feeling gooseflesh from the old Halloween prayer.

Queenie wanted to bury her face and her sorrow out of sight, but she kept on looking up into hazel eyes that appeared as dazed as she felt.

Mitchell Kingsolver.

She knew him immediately.

His eyes cleared. He blinked, and his sensitive mouth—why had she never noticed how uncertain it was—opened a little.

He blinked again, focusing on her face. "Queenie?"

"Who else would I be?"

He frowned a bit. "I was afraid—"

"*I* was afraid, darling Mitch. I thought I might have spoiled everything with my sharp words and unreasonable attitude."

He seemed about to speak, but she went on looking into his face, drinking in the sight of him. "I should have told you about the Caledonian Curse. But you should have told me about James."

His eyes narrowed.

Queenie kept her gaze on him. "I *should* have told you. You *should* have told me. And from now on, if you agree, we *shall* always tell one another the important things. James is important. He's ever so important. I love him and he loves me, but we weren't together—not the way you and I were, and the way we will be again if you agree."

He said, huskily, "I know."

"He said you would. He doesn't really want to share, because he has so little, and he knows *you* don't want to share . . . but you see, that puts us three in a fix. I wish we could all be happy . . . Now—can you get us out of our fix?"

His arms tightened around her, and he bent and gave her a long kiss.

"I'll do my darnedest, my love." He looked down at her again with a faint smile. "It's not altruism."

"No, dear Mitch. It's what you do."

Chapter Twenty-one: Mitchell Kingsolver Redux

Queenie Hart, November 1st, 2021

"Happy birthday, by the way."

Queenie smiled at Mitch across the kitchen table in The Belfry.

She was weary, but she couldn't give in to sleep. Not yet.

Her fears that Mitch would return stark naked were unfounded. By the time the lights came on at the ball, he was dressed in his familiar muted clothing, which Queenie recognised as being the colour of eucalyptus leaves.

After the first reorientation, he assumed his driver's cap, and, holding Queenie by the hand, he went to the door of Oakengrove to watch the departing guests.

"Anyone for Borrow Junction?" he asked as they passed. "Or for Fiddle Bay?"

"Us," Kez said. She grinned at him. "Lovely to see you again, Mitch. Are you and James going to duke it out to see who gets to drive Ethel?"

"Not tonight, Kez." Mitch pushed his cap back. "James had to go, but he wants you to know he'll be back next year."

"He'd better bring that kilt," another of the Chess-Nuts said brightly. "What do you think of Queenie's brilliant costume?"

"Pity you weren't here earlier to give us a spin on the floor," Kez added.

"Couldn't be helped. Anyway, what about your arthritis?"

"I think a man in a kilt makes a grand antidote to Arthur Ritis," Kez said. She gave her trademark cackle. "Saving your pardon, Mitch — you know I love you too."

"I did catch the end of the dance with Queenie," Mitch said.

"Well, James has been keeping her warm for you," Kez said slyly.

Mitch said, agreeably, "I know, and he'd better have done a good job of it."

Kez, for the first time since Queenie had known her, looked disconcerted.

He drove the Chess-Nuts back to their stops, then, without discussion, he drove Queenie and her besom back to The Belfry.

Hence they now sat in her kitchen, holding hands across the table.

"You look highly desirable in that costume," Mitch said. "Delicious, I might add. By far the best advertising I've ever seen."

It trembled on Queenie's mind to say, "Aye?" in a tart voice, but instead she said, "Thank you. I bought it from a boutique called Fairings. Happy birthday, by the way." She smiled at him.

"Thank you. I won't ask you how you know."

"About James," Queenie said after a few moments.

"We need to talk about him. You were right, we *should* have talked before."

"Can we now?"

"It's late."

"As if I could sleep now!" she snapped.

"Okay." He took an audible breath. "*He has so little.* You said that. I know that. It hurts."

"Is that why you don't want to talk about him?"

He gave a small nod. "Would you?"

188

"Maybe not. I don't talk about my lassie haggis Caledonian Curse problem."

"Tell me about that."

She told him. "So that's one reason I was so unkind and unjust to you that last day. It's a reason, but not an excuse. I *can* control it if I focus hard, but I get weary and sometimes I just let it have its head."

"James didn't mind it."

"No — until I asked if you were his spaniel bitch. Or was it the other way around."

"Ouch."

"Cue hissy fit in broad Glaswegian," she said.

"He did get rather vehement," he said. "He doesn't usually." He looked directly into Queenie's eyes. "It was the Queenie effect. *To see you is to love you, to be exasperated, and yet to love you still.*"

"Yes. I know I can be exasperating, but I have it on good authority that I have a right to ask for what I want . . . and even to wish for it. The *to see you* thing works with you two for me. James is exactly my type — in October, especially."

"I'm not?" He sounded wistful rather than hurt.

"You are also exactly my type." She shrugged. "So I'm greedy. I love your face, and your hands. Under your clothes, you're pretty much perfect."

"But you can't remember my face."

Queenie laughed delightedly. "But I can! I remembered you as soon as the lights came up! I felt James hand the baton to you, and your face came into my mind while you were kissing me. I'll never forget it now."

He kept looking into her eyes, and his own were reflective. "The change felt different this time . . . Better. Gentle."

"I'm glad."

"It was because of you. Because you gave James something to hold on to, he — passed the baton, as you put it."

"He didn't have any choice," Queenie said.

"Oh, doesn't he just! He can choose to try to hold on. It doesn't work, but I feel it. The first few days after the transition can be — rough."

"And the last few days beforehand?" she asked.

He nodded. "Especially last time. I hated to go with you not knowing . . . maybe not caring . . ."

She leaned forwards. "But ye know . . ." She caught herself up sharply. "You do know what James and I worked out."

"Yes — broadly speaking. You decided we should share you . . . with good grace. And if that can't happen, then *we* can't happen."

"It's not a threat," she said.

"I understand that. Queenie, I know I need to fix this, but it can't be forced. I learned that from the time I tried to help the widow. It took much longer than I hoped and expected."

"But you did fix it — her."

He shook his head. "I thought I did, but I think perhaps she fixed herself when she was ready."

"But you supported her until she could do that." She dropped her gaze to their joined hands.

"What are you thinking?"

"That time was hard for James," she said.

"I know." He squeezed her hands gently. "I thought at the time . . . well, you just have to wear it, mate, same as *I* have to put up with argyle sweaters in my closet at the *pied-a-terre*. But I did know that was unfair. I pretty much decided not to do that kind of fixing again."

"You object to his argyle sweaters?"

"Great bogle, Queenie, love — don't you? They're . . ." Words seemed to fail him.

"Bizarre? Eye-catching? Eccentric?" She laughed. "Poor wee Mitchell. If ye cannae stand the argyle, wha' do ye make o' *me*?"

She released his hands, got up, and stalked around the table. "Scroosh back, mun. I need a wee bitty snuggle."

Mitch pushed his chair back, and he opened his arms.

Queenie turned, the back portion of her skirt swishing in a satisfying manner, and then she sat down in his lap. She took a few seconds to squirm into a comfortable position.

When she was sure she'd achieved her effect, she relaxed against him with a sigh of satisfaction. "Well?" she said.

Mitch laughed. "You know very well I would do anything for you."

"But I'm brash, sometimes very rude, and I have a radged braewoman armed with a besom in me," she said.

"Mainly in October."

"Aye, but she's still here. If I let my guard down . . ." That didn't sound quite right.

Mitch gave her a hug. "Queenie, I think maybe you're *letting* her have her say now, rather than being unable to suppress her."

"I think you're right. It's gey satisfying noo and then."

"I'm sure it is. And I *will* try to acknowledge James as a part of my life."

"Our lives," she corrected gently.

"Our lives."

Queenie kissed him. "We've talked enough for tonight. Will you come to bed with me?"

"Need you ask?"

"Yes. I do need to. I won't ever assume."

At that point, all hell broke loose in the belltower.

CHAPTER TWENTY-TWO: BATS OUT OF THE BELFRY

Queenie Hart, November 1st, 2021

"What the feck is that?"

Queenie frowned as she listened to squeaking, twittering, flapping and fluttering, silent booming growing to a tinging and then to a ringing until the cacophony reached a pitch where normal speech could not be heard.

She surged up from Mitch's lap, bringing a gasp from him that she couldn't hear.

She seized her besom and she stalked to the narthex, where she beat a rapid tattoo on the door.

"Wheesht! Be still, thou unmannerly furry wee fiendies!" she commanded.

Silence fell and then came a defiant jangling boom and an enormous burst of fluttering wings.

Mitch grasped Queenie by the hand and ran her down the steps and out into the moonlight.

The half moon rode in rifts of clouds, and Mitch turned Queenie and pointed up at the belltower. "Look!"

Queenie looked.

Boiling out of the tower, from some unseen gap in the stones, separating briefly around the cross before recombining, poured a tribe of bats, flitting, swooping, and whirling away across the moon, then streaming off in the direction of Fiddle Bay.

Queenie stared in mounting delight. "Och, *look* at them, Jamie!"

She caught herself up in an instant. "Oh . . . Mitch . . ."

He tightened his arm around her. "I'm sure he sees them . . . So do I."

They watched until the bats vanished into the night.

"Where are they going?" Queenie asked.

"I expect they're heading for the cove gateway," Mitch said.

"The . . ."

"There's a cave at one end of the cove that's a gateway to *over there*. It's a tricky one to negotiate, because of the tides, but I've used it quite often, and bats would have no trouble."

Queenie silently absorbed one more wonder and the answer to a few more unasked questions.

"Let's go to bed," she said abruptly.

They went back into The Belfry. Queenie indicated the warded door.

"Oliver Porthwellian is coming tomorrow to open that for us. Andy's bringing him. Oliver said if he were sixty years younger and a single man, he'd lay me well. Andy is the one who told me I had a right to be exasperating. You'll be able to meet them both over a cup of tea and tarts *after* Oliver has let me into the belltower. And by the way, Oliver said my swain might help me to clear up the lingering bat shite. He meant James, I think, but now *you* can fix it."

"I can't wait," Mitch said, in the driest voice she had ever heard him use. He bent to kiss her temple.

They went up the stairs to the mezzanine bedroom, where Queenie removed her finery. She gave it an affectionate pat and then she folded it away in her chest.

She glanced at James's childhood, packed away in the basket by her bed. That could wait.

She considered the fay ice queen, Ayesha, and her anti-

James proclivities. That, too, could wait.

She raised her hands to take off the beautiful thistle necklace.

Mitch stopped her. "Leave it on, my darling. Mum obviously wants you to have it."

"I will, then."

She picked up the *aide-mémoire*. "I won't need this anymore for facial recognition, but Mitch . . . I'll be getting some prints from Maureen Tucker in the next few days."

"You and James at the ball," he said.

"Yes. Later today, I want you to come with me to get her to take one of us, too . . . if you like."

"Anything for you, my love."

"Yes. Well." Queenie got into bed and then she turned her full attention to Mitch. "Get naked for me?"

His smile lit his face, and he double tapped his wrist.

His clothing vanished.

"You're ready," she remarked.

"I can wait."

She pouted. "*I* can't. But before we get down to it, there's something else I promised James."

Mitch sighed. "I see my troublesome silent partner is planning to be more troublesome than ever. He *has* been busy."

"He has a right to be busy."

"I know."

"And he needs a dog."

"I see."

"And possibly babies."

"What — when?"

"When it's time. And that means we're going to have to sort things with Ayesha."

"We are? But what exactly have you promised James? What have you two been plotting?"

"Nothing bad. But sometimes when I'm snuggling up with

you, I'm going to spare a thought for James and how much I love my laddie. I was doing the same for you when we decided . . . I almost thought I felt *you* kissing me once."

Mitch went silent, but it didn't feel hostile to Queenie. Eventually, he said, "How about giving him a bit of what he needs now? That way, when you come to me, I'll know you really are *with* me."

It wasn't the most gracious concession, but it was a start.

Queenie put her arms around Mitch. "I'm going to imagine ye in pyjamas," she said. She put her lips close to his. "Jamie, darling laddie, this one is for you." She kissed Mitch. He stiffened, but after a few seconds she felt his barriers give way, and she smelled clean wool.

She took her time, holding her braw laddie in her mind's eye until he moved gently away, leaving her clasped tightly in Mitch's arms.

"Queenie—I can't wait—" he said urgently.

"Anything for me, you said," she retorted, then her body took over and she scrambled over on top of him.

He was so stiff and she was so ready they were coupled up in a second, clasped and kissing, gasping and then yelling out with exultation.

Queenie's head spun.

She flopped on top of Mitch, still hanging on, and kissed his face all over.

He laughed, sliding one hand down to a possessive clasp on her bottom.

"You know what I would really like now, my queen?"

"What?" she asked, wriggling her hips.

"Tarts. Lots of tarts. A great many tarts . . ."

"Oh, really! And I expect you want me to go and get them."

"No, my love . . . if you permit."

"Oh, go ahead. They're in the fridge—lawks!" She froze. "It's Sunday, and I forgot Oliver's wee order!"

"It's Monday, actually," Mitch said. He handed her a soft cloth for mopping up, and Queenie hastily applied it.

"Och . . ." She wanted to sleep, but she got out of bed, pulled on a gown and hurried to assemble the forgotten tarts in the tureen.

She set them on the table with a sigh, and then she took the remaining Queen of Hearts back to Mitch.

He consumed it with evident pleasure.

She lay down again and curled against her pixie lover, regardless of the crumbs and the fact he was licking his fingers.

Mitch put his arms around her and gave her a sticky kiss.

Queenie purred, which unfortunately brought someone else to mind.

Bother — that darned ice queen.

And Oliver and Andy will be here in a few hours.

I hope Dellion comes too.

I hope Oliver's not too cranky about the delay in his order.

Jamie, it's going to be all right.

I wish ye could hae stayed to see the bells. Next time . . .

Lawks! Mum and Dad will be calling me first thing! Whatever will I say?

She sighed. Her parents always called her the day *after* her birthday, on account of the Curse—even though they didn't believe in it.

What to do . . . what to do . . .

Och, dinnae fash, lassie. Ye ken fine it will work oot for ye. Are ye no' the Queen of Tarts? Aye? Then get to tarting!

She squirmed round and licked Mitch's shoulder as a statement of intention.

"Hm?" he said.

"However did you get jam up there? Och—never mind. Mitchell Kingsolver, I'm in a fix."

"Another one?"

"Aye. I need to quiet my mind so I can sleep."

"You need me to meditate with you? Or rub your back? I

could do that."

"No, Mitch—I need you to *ravish* me and send me out of my mind to stop the questions bothering me. Can you do that?"

"Anything for you, my love . . . and this time, I'm going on top!"

ABOUT THE AUTHOR

Lark Westerly lives in the island state of Tasmania.

Like Queenie Hart, she often thinks Obsession might be her extra middle name. Some of her obsessions include creating worlds, lists of interesting names, walking the dogs, reading, and pursuing whatever research might support her current project. For Queen of Tarts, she read up on Scottish dogs, the expenses involved in hiring a piper, Cornish names, Picts, brocade, Scottish slang, English names, name frequency tables, church terminology, kilts and their accompaniments, argyle sweaters, besoms, and Scotch broth. She had a great deal of fun meeting old friends, and being quite startled to realise that telephoning Dellion Tredennick, eating tarts with Queenie and buying a costume from Fairings after a visit to the O-Quay Café really wasn't on the cards tomorrow.

She *has* been to Circular Quay, but there wasn't a living statue, and he didn't give her a wish. Neither has she ever had bats in her belfry . . . as far as she knows.

www.ingramcontent.com/pod-product-compliance
Lightning Source LLC
Chambersburg PA
CBHW060056150626
46556CB00017BA/848

* 9 7 8 1 4 8 7 4 3 4 5 4 0 *